VALKYRIE UPRISING

VALKYRIE ALLEGIANCE BOOK 3

A.J. FLOWERS

GLOSSARY OF NORSE MYTHOLOGICAL TERMS

This is a work of fiction and any relation to Norse Mythology is the author's creative interpretation.

This glossary contains major spoilers meant to be revealed in the story, but like all Immortals, you have the option of peering into the future... at your own risk.

EVENTS

Ragnarök: A final battle between gods that will result in death and rebirth.

PLANETS

Asgard: The original home world of the Immortals created by Odin, now under control by Baldr.

Muspelheim: A volcanic planet that lies outside of time and space. Originally a planet belonging to the Surtr, Freya has taken residence after her alliance with the Jotun to rebuild her armies and take back Asgard from Baldr.

Earth: The birthplace of the gods.

IMMORTALS:

Freya: Goddess of War who has allied with her other half, Odin, as well as the Jotun. Before her exile from Asgard, she was better known as the goddess of love, beauty, and passion.

Odin: A cyborg who became the first Immortal and is now a ruthless warlord and God of War alongside his wife. Exiled from Asgard, he fights to defend his honor and return to Asgard, the planet he created for Immortals.

Baldr: Freya's only son and once loved by the gods, Baldr has exiled his parents from Asgard and is determined to bring about Ragnarök.

Tyr (Mortal Name: Tyler): One of the Valiant and top lieutenants in Odin's army. Has a mysterious connection with Valarie Frigg and often calls her Aerie, likely referring to a past she can't remember.

William Johnson: Recently ascended mortal and one of Odin's newest soldiers of the Valiant.

Heimdall: Now known as Dalia, Heimdall is a defected exile of Asgard and now prominent stock broker and Immortal arm's dealer in New York. Her powers center in farsight: seeing events up to a hundred miles from her current location, allowing her to establish a stronghold in New York where nothing happens without her knowledge.

SPACESHIPS

Einherjar: One of the major spaceships that is capable of bending time and space. The Einherjar belongs to the immortal Freya and is powered by human souls and is the birthplace of her daughters.

Mojinir: Odin's spaceship that can destroy entire planets when fully charged.

Sleipnir: A satellite that serves to transport Immortals between planets, built by Odin.

Gulltop: Heimdall's ship that relocates the Bifrost, the

only entrance to Asgard controlled by Heimdall. Gulltop is located on the dark side of the moon.

Jotunheim: A ship buried in the caverns of Muspelheim and long argued to be the birthplace of the Jotun. A scientist by the name of Ymir wanted to explore the idea of reverse terraforming. Instead of adapting a planet to the race... adapt the race to the planet.

RACES

Valkyrie: Immortal daughters of Freya. Divisions of Freya's army include Frigg, Lofin, Fulla, and Gina, each with their subtle strengths and talents. Frigg are benders of time. Lofin are healers. The Fulla guide the creation of the Valkyrie. The Gina are best around water and cannot survive long on Muspelheim.

The Valiant: Human souls who have earned their immortality by pledging eternal service to Odin after their first kill. Only humans who have been dedicated to the Norn and achieved reincarnation will have the opportunity to kill an Immortal as the necessary sacrifice to ascend themselves.

Skuld: Servants to the Norn. Shadowed remnants of souls neither living nor dead. They only know how to feed on the life-force of Immortals. In exchange for their service, the Norns provide sustenance and rejuvenation to keep their withered bodies in one piece.

Norn: Ancient Valkyries who've lost their way and now work to control the fates of men and gods. When a mortal soul is offered, they feed off of sacrifice, locking that soul into a cycle of reincarnation until it can ascend. Valkyries will often target souls dedicated to the Norn to take the soul after its final sacrifice to the Einherjar where it will serve as a power source. Souls that succeed in defeating the Valkyrie come to claim them ascend as one of the Valiant.

THE JOTUN

Jotun: A collective of elementals who ally themselves with Freya. The Jotun consist of the Surtr, Skaoi, Huldra, and other undiscovered races who are adept at adapting to their surroundings, eventually evolving into the element most akin to the planet they call home.

Surtr: Fiery Embers, natives of Muspelheim and spirits who've allied themselves with Freya.

Skaoi: Ice elementals.

Huldra: Forest Spirits who dwell on Earth and have a shaky alliance with Freya.

ARTIFICIAL INTELLIGENCE PROGRAMS

Thor: An AI program that resets human memories in realtime.

Jormungand: Thor believes it will one day malfunction and become Jormungand, represented as the serpent eternally devouring its own tail. The malfunction is predicted to result in a poisoned sky that will rain terror on the world during Ragnarök.

Grimhildr: Housed in Freya's spear, the Grimhildr program suppresses memories and unleashes rings of flame in battle, confusing enemies. It keeps a record of the memories it has seen and grows unstable when Freya tries to use it on Val a second time.

Yggdrasil: The origin of immortality. The energy of souls are converted to a physical substance called "Yggdrasil's Sap", or YS, that creates life. Yggdrasil's core is held on Asgard but is linked to all major spaceships, allowing the creation of new life and the sharing of the Sap of Yggdrasil.

Third Law of the Valkyrie...

Don't Trigger Ragnarök

CHAPTER 1

Ragnarök

*E*mbers floated across a barren landscape and even though I had power over time and space, that moment stilled on its own. The heat wavered dusty air and my gaze settled onto a staggering Valkyrie with withered wings. She limped and growled, half her flesh replaced with the glittering scourge of Ragnarök's dark power. She drew it in with great, gulping breaths as she continued to stumble across ash and lingering flames. Sam's glassy eyes reflected my horrified face as she came close enough that the putrid stench of decay and ash tinged my nose. She bared her teeth and growled.

This wasn't Sam. She'd lost all the snark and grace I loved about her. This was a shell of what was left.

Darkness filtered through her skin and seeped from her eyes, leaking across her defined cheekbones like a war tattoo. I reached out to touch her, but stopped short when the icy chill of Ragnarök's harsh kiss grazed my mortal fingertips like razor blades.

It was Will who finally brought me back. His fingers dug into my shoulder and forced me to fall back against his hard chest. My gaze lingered on my lost sister and I scrunched my eyebrows at the soft yearning that wrapped around my soul.

Ragnarök wanted to draw me in with the rest of my sisters it had already claimed. In an instant, I knew what it wanted and a deep, primal part of me yearned for it to succeed. In order for there to be life, there must be death. Like my sisters, new life could rise from the ashes. Worlds would be reborn and given a fresh slate. Ragnarök had achieved that thrice before, the lore retold through generations by the Valkyries who had survived the end of the world. Freya was one of the only ones and she'd tell me those nightmarish bedtime stories as a warning. Even if Ragnarök ended our world, the suffering wouldn't dissipate. And so it devoured the darkness until it had become a sentient being. It stared back at me through my fallen sister's eyes and for a brief moment, its heart touched mine.

Then Will whispered my name and pulled me back from the brink. "Val," he said, his voice a pin drop in the silent room of my heart.

I turned away from the draw of glittering darkness. This was my reality. Tyler half-dead at my feet. William's eyes alight with panic. And darkness seeping up from the grainy sands of Muspelheim that were about to take us under.

I closed my eyes and concentrated. I was a Frigg and a daughter of two gods. I knew the extent of my powers now and the source of my strength.

Love.

It's what my mother had feared. It's what had given Ragnarök a window to enter into our world, and it's what would save Tyler and Will so that we could fight it together.

When I opened my eyes again, I blinked as a cool blast of recycled air swept my hair over my shoulders. A ship's ancient groans sounded along the abused hull. I scented the rot of Ragnarök in the air. I'd slipped through time and space, bringing Tyler and Will with me to the Einherjar.

I knelt and swept my hands over their mouths to make sure they were still breathing. They didn't move, but soft puffs against my fingertips told me that they'd survived. Will glowed with the protective hue of Odin's power, while Tyler glimmered with dark runes visible to the naked eye, betraying his Heimdall connection to the mysterious matter that made up of turmoil and darkness, I scented the rot of Ragnarök's power.

Pain and suffering was the weight that drove Ragnarök. It's what gave Tyler his strength, and even though I had the same gifts, I was a Frigg. Love was my strength. Time and space warped when I commanded it to, but to bring others with me broke more than just the laws of physics. There were the three laws of the Valkyrie... and then there were the unspoken rules of the universe.

I shivered and stood as I hugged myself. Who cares what new law I'd broken? I should be used to it by now.

My memories were on my side for once, letting me

know that this ship lazily orbited Muspelheim and kept its eternal watch over my Immortal sisters. I'd landed on the viewing deck where'd I'd spent hours just staring at Muspelheim before I was old enough to live there.

I turned to find a broad wall of glass separating me from the void of space. A horizon view showed me the Einherjar reluctantly drifting away from my home. I could see why. Glittering black jaws closed in around the ruby world and threatened to swallow it whole.

"No," I whispered as tears sprang to my eyes. Muspelheim thrummed with its heat and red gleam like a beacon in the universe. I couldn't imagine it being snuffed out, along with all the Valkyries who lived there and trained for the final battle. Most of my life, I'd just wanted to be a part of them and make them proud. Now, that final battle was here, and they hadn't been ready… because of me.

"You shouldn't be here," a warning voice said from the end of the room.

I whirled and tears flung from my face. "Mother?" I asked.

She seemed smaller in person as if the trials of the end

of the world had diminished her greatness, but she straightened and kept a tight grip on her spear. Ash drifted down her dress, betraying that she'd recently summoned her wings. She loved her daughters, even if she wouldn't admit it. I couldn't imagine what this was doing to her and I wanted to run and hug her and tell her that it'd all somehow be all right. Love was what gave her the purest white wings I'd ever seen and I wanted to have that part of her back. Yet, it was the look on her face that rooted me where I stood.

"You're beyond redemption," she snarled and her eyes flashed with a ruby gleam, burying any hope that I'd reclaimed the goddess of love I knew her to be. Freya stood before me now, the scorned goddess of war. She stabbed the butt of her spear to the ground and the sharp echo against the ship's hull made me wince. "You've broken all three laws of the Valkyrie. Was that not enough? Now you shred through time and space, bringing your toys with you?" Her gaze fell to the two Valiant warriors at my feet.

A flash of gold brilliance came to life at her side and made her startle. The motion put me on edge and all the hairs along my arms stood on end. The goddess of war was not easily frightened.

The father of the Valiant appeared as a hologram,

magic mixed with technology, and glimmered with eerie translucence as he took in the scene. His mechanical left arm whirred as he clenched a fist. "Why are two of my soldiers asleep on your deck?" he growled.

I realized that he'd addressed Freya and not me. "Father?" I asked, wishing I could wipe out the pathetic waver of my voice. If he was going to yell at anyone, it should be me. Freya had an entire planet to worry about.

He continued to ignore me and turned the full wrath of his gaze on Freya. "How could you have allowed this to happen? I thought you said that you had things under control?"

Freya's lower lip trembled and she clamped down on it hard before lashing out her reply. "She's just as much your daughter as mine. Perhaps that's why she's so attached to those fools she's brought with her." Embers streaked through her immortal body, evidence of the power of flame that coursed through her veins. Sweat broke out on my forehead and I wiped it away. I'd almost forgotten that I still had my mortal body.

As if sensing my distress, Freya turned to me. "Why

did you bring them?" Her words cut off short as if my answer terrified her.

I swallowed. "Because… I love them."

Both Odin and Freya, deities of war and wrath, stared at me as if I'd just broken their hearts.

TYLER'S SECRETS

Freya left me alone with the two sleeping Valiant and a view of the destruction my love had wrought. I sat cross-legged as I watched the glittering grains of Ragnarök seep through a rip in space and time, its fingers slowly wrapping around the ruby planet like a snake constricting its prey.

I don't know how long I sat there, but it was long enough for Freya's embers to have retreated and the mournful darkness to wrap the chamber in a cold chill. I didn't notice that I shivered until Will wrapped an arm around me from behind and hugged me to his chest. I leaned into him and didn't try to stop the fresh tears that bubbled up. I'd thought that I was all cried out, but he seemed to awaken something in me that was buried so deep, it broke through fresh love and pain.

Tyler had awakened as well, but he didn't complain at the protective hold Will had on me. He straddled me with his legs and pulled me to him and hugged me tight. His cheek pressed against mine and he just held me, and I knew he'd be there for me as long as I needed.

Tyler sat across from me and took my hand in his. I couldn't believe that he'd be so kind to me when Will was right here, but his features didn't hold any jealousy or anger. His crystal eyes went soft as he stroked his thumb over my knuckles. "I'm sorry," he said, his voice a low, husky whisper.

Will hugged me tighter. His breath puffed on my neck as he spoke. "Val?"

I shifted and snuggled into the crook of his arm, keeping Tyler's hand in mine. "Yes?"

He glanced at Tyler, as if for the first time acknowledging his rival was there. Yet, he didn't look annoyed or angry. Instead, a whisper of a smile tugged at his lips. "I'm glad you saved us."

Tyler shook his head. "It's not worth the price." He glanced at the span of destruction through the viewing shield. "Ragnarök has staked its claim and nothing can stop it now."

I didn't want to face that horrible truth. This couldn't be the end of the universe.

I chose to study the harsh, beautiful lines of Tyler's face. The attack on Muspelheim had torn at his armor, leaving it to stick itself back together as if an invisible seamstress worked her needles before my eyes. The gashes left open revealed hard abs and the bulge of his bicep tearing through the fabric. His skin still boasted the dark runes, but they flickered against the golden sheen of power that draped over him like a soft aura. I looked down to my own stretched mark that had hardened on my hand. "Is this why you became a Valiant?" I asked. I hesitated, then ran my fingers over the gold film that drifted over his skin. "Odin keeps it at bay, doesn't he?"

He stared at me for a moment, then nodded. "I'm a Heimdall. I think you know what that means now."

I didn't know what it meant, not entirely. All I knew was that his mother was the caretaker of the Bifrost. That was the only place where time and space didn't have rules.

Will stroked my arms as if trying to banish the chill that refused to leave my bones. "The echoes of Ragnarök," Will said. His words came out distant as if he were piecing a puzzle together. "What if that darkness settled into souls?"

Tyler stiffened. "Yes," he said. "You're getting warmer, lover boy."

A new kind of chill ran down my spine. I covered the black rune on my hand, wishing I could banish it from my body. "Ragnarök is here because of us."

Tyler nodded. "Right again."

I thought that I'd been the harbinger of Ragnarök, but it wasn't just me. It was those I loved, and my love was drawn to others like me.

I turned to Will and frowned. While he didn't have dark runes, he'd only recently become Immortal. He had experienced more darkness than I cared to admit, a byproduct of his time trapped under the Norn's curse.

Tyler stood and offered his hand. "Can I show you something?"

When I glanced at Will, he smiled his encouragement. Somehow, the two had formed a bond and were on the same side. I guess they had a point. With the universe about to end, there wasn't much purpose in fighting over a girl.

I took Tyler's hand and he led me down the hall. Will remained behind. He clasped his hands behind his back and gazed out of the viewing shield, surveying the damage that we'd done. As Tyler eased me around the corner, I thought I caught a wisp of shadow licking at Will's fingertips.

I sensed Freya and Odin, but I had no doubt they were off arguing whose fault it was that I'd triggered Ragnarök. Leaving me with Will and Tyler meant they knew I was in good hands. Even though my parents had forbidden me to love, it gave me a small comfort that they trusted those I'd given my heart.

As Tyler guided me down the halls, I realized that we'd been holding hands this whole time. It felt so much easier to love now that the threat of Ragnarök had already come to fruition. Even though the end of the world should have terrified me—and it did—I indulged the forbidden pleasure to allow myself to do something I'd never done before. I was allowed to *feel*.

Tyler smirked at me. "You're staring."

A blush heated my cheeks. "I know." I squeezed his

hand and he stopped. I didn't care if he knew how I felt now that I'd already broken all of the rules.

"What about Will?" he asked, his mischievous tone turning serious. "He loves you. It'd take a blind man not to see that."

I nodded. "And I think I love him too."

Tyler winced at that admission. "Okay, then, why are you looking at me like I'm your knight in shining armor?"

I swallowed hard before pulling him closer. My fingers ran up the strength of his arms and flattened against his chest. His heart thundered under my fingertips. "Is it possible that I could love you both?"

He blinked, his crystal eyes flitting between the magics of Odin and Heimdall, resulting in a rainbow of gold and black. The effect mesmerized me. "I think you know how I feel about you, Aerie." As if against his will, he curled me closer and his fingers ran through my hair. He had no reason to fight his feelings anymore, but something sent his jaw flexing before he spoke again. "The difference between us is I know why you might love me, and it's not because of who I am." In spite of the sting of his rejection, his lips came closer, the prickle of ice and magic sprinkling over my entire body as his desire filtered through. "You love *what* I am."

"What if you're wrong?" I asked. I drifted closer to him, closing the minuscule distance between us. I hesitated when his breath caressed my face, but he didn't pull away. I gave in to the need to taste him until our lips met.

His entire body went stiff, then he curled into the kiss as his tongue grazed against mine, suddenly passionate as if I'd managed to flip a switch off his resistance to me. His presence engulfed me, hot and hungry. He gave me that brief moment to know him and the passion he was capable of before the magic between us shut off with a snap. He pushed me away as darkness clouded over his eyes until only a terrifying void remained. I couldn't see the crystal or the spark of his beauty. There was only a glassy black that came from within his soul and glazed over the love he held for me. "Ragnarök isn't the worst that could happen," he warned.

I swallowed hard. I'd always known that Tyler had a secret. "What could possibly be worse than Ragnarök?" I didn't want to be afraid of him. There was a kindred connection between me and the darkness that brought his runes to life across his skin. His armor threatened to disintegrate as it became translu-cent, giving me a blush-worthy view of his perfect body.

"This is a darkness that threatens to consume me. I've survived it, but at a cost. I would not have you pay that cost."

I ran my fingers across his cheek. No matter what he was, he was beautiful to me. "Does it hurt?" I knew he wouldn't tell me what it cost him to keep the madness that overtook the Norn out of his eyes, but I could sense the deep weight of suffering in him.

He leaned into my touch and closed his eyes. "You're drawn to me because my bloodline is a direct lineage of the power that fuels Ragnarök." His eyes flashed open, somehow a deeper shade of black than they'd been before. "To love me is to reject peace. So many would die if you and I..." His words drifted off.

I forced myself to let my hand fall. "If I chose you," I finished for him. There was a reason I found my heart belonging to both Will and Tyler. They represented two distinct futures and I had yet to make my choice.

Tyler emanated darkness and chaos, a boon of the Heimdall line. He was the true descendant of the power that kept souls permanently bound to this world. Darkness, suffering, and pain were what prevented a soul from returning to Yggdrasil. That power shone through him and sang each trait with glaring realization. I found its significance when I looked into his eyes. Without it, there would be no life at all. There would be nothing to ground new souls to this plane and life would never have started in the first place. I drifted closer as I admired him.

Immortality. Strength. Beauty. *Terror.*

"You cannot choose me," he growled. He grabbed my hand and tugged me along with him. "Perhaps if you see it, you'll come to your senses." He glowered at me over his shoulder. "I cannot fight what I feel for you if you are not fighting it too."

Panic surged in me as Tyler all but sprouted wings and flew down the constricting halls of the Einherjar. We took twisted turns, going through airlock walls that flew open at our passing and sent fresh blasts of cold air over my face.

When we reached a chamber with winding pipes and a low melody that I recognized from a distant memory, I forced Tyler to stop. "I know that song."

Tyler released me and I wandered closer to a door that vaulted all the way to a two-story ceiling. This was the center of the Einherjar and I'd only been here once before. I couldn't remember what was on the other side of this door, but it both enthralled and terrified me.

"You should," Tyler said. "It's the song of Yggdrasil."

Heartbreak was the only description for the way this song made me feel. "Why is it so sad?" I asked as I ran my fingers over the crystals embedded into the door. Pipes surrounded the frame as they twisted over one another and delved into the floor. Mechanical groans and hissing sounded when I stepped on the thin panels that separated the ship from the contents of the chamber beyond.

"It's a lamentation," he explained and pressed on the crystals. Unlike me, they came to life under his touch. The walls rumbled, and then the door began a slow ascent.

I fumbled with my tattered clothes as I waited. "Does Freya know we're here?" I asked. This was her ship, and if my memory was right, this was the Einherjar's core. We were definitely not allowed to be here.

Tyler shrugged. "I'm shielding us. If she's monitoring us, then she thinks we're still on the viewing deck with Will."

I blinked at him. "Really?" My gaze swept over him again, taking in the sizzle of magic that hummed under the golden sheen of Odin's light. He was working the dark magic of Heimdall, and that both enthralled and terrified me. "Is that safe?"

He glanced at me. "No, but you must see this, and Freya wouldn't allow it."

The door fully raised, then he stepped inside. I drew in a deep breath and followed.

EINHERJAR'S CORE

*U*nlike the honeycomb of tattered souls I'd found in the Huldra's nest, Einherjar's core was full of life and wonder. Orbs swirled around twining roots of a giant tree that spanned up into an impossibly long core that speared through the center of the Einherjar.

"This must go through the entire ship," I said, my neck arched back as I stared upward in awe. I'd always imagined the core of the Einherjar to be like any other spaceship which was a singular ball of light and plasma. The Mojinir and the other smaller ships that ferried the Valkyrie to the various outlier planets had such cores. But this? I ran my fingers through the fine mist of the air that tingled with life and mystery. I'd never felt anything like it.

Tyler frowned and reached out to grab my fingers and lowered my hand to my side. "Don't be deceived. These souls suffer. They'll never move on to the real Yggdrasil."

I blinked at him. He still watched me with that eerie black gaze. I didn't like it when the darkness overcame him. It felt like he was cut off from me. "These are the souls that my sisters have reaped."

Tyler nodded and took my hand, guiding me down the silver path to the center of the tree. Great, winding roots walled in around us and pierced the metallic hull. That's what the pipes were for. The roots spanned the entirety of the ship.

Tyler tugged me close as souls whispered by us. Slight stings radiated across my arm where the faint blue power ran over us. Tyler shrouded me with his darkness and soothed the faint hurt. "Souls trapped by the Norn's curse can't make their way back to Yggdrasil," he said, keeping his voice low. "I can't approve what the Norn do to them. Eventually souls are destroyed under the weight of their dark magic. But Freya's version of the afterlife for such lost souls isn't much better." He forced my hand onto the rough bark of the tree's lower trunk. I flinched as raw power tingled through my mortal skin and grazed the Valkyrie embers in my soul… as well as my own darkness.

I closed my eyes as the voices filtered in. Young men through the ages who'd suffered under the hands of the Norn, and now were trapped in this place until they too would be torn apart, not to feed the Norn's lust for eternal life, but to feed Freya's need for vengeance against them and her desire to create her daughters. My sisters, I realized as a chill swept through me, were recycled bits of these souls and sorrows.

My eyes flung open and Tyler released me. I couldn't look at him. Instead, I gazed up at the span of streaking light that glimmered through the tree. My mother used these souls, and no matter her reasoning, the end did not justify the means. "What can I do to fix this?"

Will's booming voice was my answer through the forbidden chamber. "You break me free of Odin's bond so that I can tear this abomination down myself."

I whirled to find Will marching towards us. Shadows whispered at his fingertips and left a trail of smoke along his footsteps. Tyler was not the only one who boasted dark magic. Will had suffered under the Norn and survived. Perhaps all Valiant had the darkness at their core. It's why Odin's power of light was so useful to them.

Will growled as an invisible wall hit him and he crashed to his knees. Sweat broke out on his brow and a snap sounded through the air. Tyler cursed, and I knew that his shield over us had banished with Will's attempt to intrude on the sacred chamber.

"Fools!" Freya's voice boomed and Valkyries appeared at her side. They filtered into the mist and souls screeched their rage at the winged abominations that had destroyed kindred souls. The blue lights dove and left searing scars along my sister's faces. They growled and swatted at them as if they were but a nuisance.

"I'm the one who brought her here," Tyler said, his voice carrying the expanse between us and my mother.

Her eyes blazed with the fires of Muspelheim. "I know, and you will pay for this. The young Valkyries are forbidden to come here."

To my surprise, Tyler smirked. "Of course. You want to make sure they're nice and brainwashed before they see what we really are."

Freya bared her teeth and pressed a sequence of buttons on her spear.

The air hummed, and then everything went black.

GROUNDED

*W*hen I awoke, it was to Freya stroking hair from my face. I sat straight up in the plush bed that threatened to engulf me with its silken sheets and goose feather stuffing. I searched the room, my memories telling me that this was my chamber on the Einherjar. My favorite obsidian statues gleamed on a shelf. Each one was a different depiction of the birds Tyler had told me about on earth. I'd been so fascinated with other creatures that had wings. It forced a smile to light my face. At the time, I'd treasured his gifts, but now I could appreciate them for what they were. Obsidian was not easily carved.

"Daughter," Freya said. The word came out smooth and apologetic.

I faced her and drew in a breath at her beauty. I couldn't remember the last time I'd been this up close to the goddess of love, for that's what she was in this moment. All the fiery rage had left her eyes, leaving them an emerald sheen that glimmered with adoration. White wings brushed at her back and her touch lingered along my arm.

Then I remembered what Tyler had shown me and I closed my heart to her. I saw her for what she really was and I leaned away.

She frowned. "Tyler should not have shown you that place."

I stiffened. Tyler hadn't placed all the blame of the horror I'd learned at Freya's feet. He'd said "we."

"Did you force Tyler to help you recruit those souls?" I don't know why he'd included himself in the admission. A Valiant couldn't recruit souls, could they?

She tried to stroke my face, but I flinched away. "He's a Heimdall. He cannot survive without feeding the darkness that torments his bloodline." She sighed. "His mother used to have an alliance with us, but it seems Baldr has offered her a better deal. I can only hope her son will not betray us as well."

My fingers dug into the sheets. "What are you talking about? What do you mean 'feeding' the darkness?"

She tilted her head and gave me a sympathetic smile as if I were so sweet and naive. "He must periodically feed on the souls we have reaped. Did he not tell you?"

The blood drained from my face. That's why Tyler had brought me there. He was going to show me why he hated himself... why I could never embrace the darkness he'd been forced to endure.

"Lies." I snapped and flung the sheets off my body. I growled to see I'd been changed into Valkyrie leathers in my sleep. They fit too snugly against my mortal curves. "Never lie to me."

She shook her head and stretched for me again, but I leaned out of her reach. "Daughter. The Norn are the villains here, not me. I only make use of their carnage for good. I take death and give it life again. Tyler has been useful to us. He's helped you manage the darkness that plagues you."

I marched to the full-length mirror and took in my appearance. Scraggly hair. A sprinkle of freckles across my face. Embers sparked at my fingertips, the Valkyrie side of me wanting to summon my spear. I indulged my rage and let the weapon come and I enjoyed the sound of surprise from Freya as she stood and fanned her wings.

"Daughter, why are you so angry?"

I didn't have time for this. Ragnarök was destroying our world and my mother was wasting time trying to justify an unpardonable sin. Perhaps Tyler had no choice, but she certainly did. I gripped my spear before turning and pointing it at her. "Where are Tyler and Will? I need to talk to them."

Her wings folded in at her back as if I'd deflated her with that statement. "You love them," she acknowledged. "I can see that. But there is a reason it is the first law among us, my daughter. Love opens up emotions that are dangerous to our kind. Love is blind. With love comes light, and with light, there is always darkness."

I frowned, but didn't lower my spear. "Ragnarök is the result of that darkness." I tilted my head. "But you already knew that."

She stared at her hands. "Yes."

"How many times have you seen Ragnarök destroy the universe?" I asked. It seemed like a ridiculous question, but instinct made me speak it aloud.

Her gaze snapped up to mine and a whisper of embers glowed in the backs of her eyes. "You are asking the wrong question."

I shook my head. "No, I think it's the right question."

The tips of her wings disintegrated, the primaries wilting and drifting ash to the floor. "You should ask me how many times I have prevented this world from being destroyed by Ragnarök." Only the goddess of war knew Ragnarök's weakness. Even speaking of it threatened to dissolve the visage of peace that stood before me now.

There was only one way that my mother knew how to stop a force as powerful as Ragnarök. "It's your fault that it exists at all," I accused. My voice shook and tears sprang to my eyes.

Her gaze darkened and the rest of her beautiful plumage turned to ash.

I didn't want to be right. Unfortunately… I was.

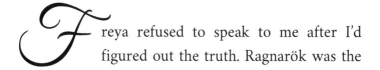reya refused to speak to me after I'd figured out the truth. Ragnarök was the

culmination of darkness drifting in the universe until it had become an angry, sentient being.

I had to know more about it. When Mama says no, try Dad.

Freya had programmed my room to stay locked, but it didn't prevent my summons of the god of war.

He appeared when I called him as a burst of golden light that sent shadows scurrying from the walls.

His rainbow eyes glittered as he appraised me. "It seems you've angered your mother," he said. His gaze went the spear that hung loosely in my grip. "Luckily yours doesn't have buttons."

I frowned. Freya tormented me with her ancient software that could do anything to a mind. She could wipe my memories, make me see things that weren't there, or just knock me out. No telling what she was doing to Will and Tyler right now.

"I need your help," I said. It was a statement, not a request, and my father straightened.

"What kind of help?"

There were a lot of things that my father could do for

me, even as his apparition, but primarily what I needed now were answers.

I rested my spear against the wall and pulled up a chair. "You never did tell me bedtime stories," I jested with a smile.

He raised a brow. A long scar streaked through it as if he'd taken a blow to the head. I remembered that my father liked his scars. It gave him character—his words, not mine.

"What kind of stories would you like to hear?" he asked.

"Ragnarök," I said immediately. "Tell me why my mother created it, and why she doesn't have the power to stop it."

He frowned, but didn't chide me for accusing my mother of such a heinous act. To my surprise, he answered me. "Your mother isn't the only one guilty of contributing to Ragnarök's current state. It is the culmination of all darkness in this universe and all the worlds that came before this one."

I bit my lip. "So you've survived Ragnarök before?"

He nodded and rubbed his mechanical arm. "Not without a price."

"Can I survive it?" I asked. I hated how hopeful I sounded. If I could survive, then maybe others could too.

Odin's gaze went distant and lines marred his face as he grimaced. "Daughter. I cannot give you hope when there is none to be had. Once Ragnarök is triggered, it will devour until it has destroyed the last of this world. Your mother and I, as well as a handful of gods, take shelter in the end days in a seed of Yggdrasil. From there, we bring forth new life. Your mother has a great burden to create life from darkness, but that was a choice we all had to make. The first time Ragnarök came for us, it was too late. When we found out its cycle, we prepared as best we could for when it would come, and put rules in place to stem off its return as long as we could."

I ran my hands over my thighs. Already my skin tingled from fighting against my Valkyrie form that threatened to break through. I couldn't lose this body. I couldn't lose hope that there could still be a chance to put things back the way they were supposed to be. "So what is Ragnarök, exactly?"

Odin's gaze remained fixated on a spot on the wall and I realized he was likely watching the glittering black fingers continue to wrap around Muspelheim. "It's the negative experiences souls have endured. Its weight cannot leave this plane. When souls leave this world behind, they shed darkness like a second skin and return to Yggdrasil. When your mother and I figured that out, we learned how to use that darkness to make ourselves Immortal. By giving the darkness form, we gave it new life."

My eyes widened. "So the two of you created Ragnarök?"

He nodded. "That's why it is our duty to keep it sated with fresh sacrifices. The Norn are a necessary evil in this world we've incidentally created. Reaped souls are valuable. They fuel our ships, create our sons and daughters, and keep Ragnarök itself at bay." His mechanical hand fisted. "We've imprisoned Ragnarök in another realm. It takes the power of the Frigg and the Bifrost working in tandem to pull the creature outside of its realm. When you opened yourself up to love, you created a fissure in the space-time web, and allowed it back in."

I snatched my spear and pointed it at him. "Don't you dare try to blame me for the destruction of the universe." That was a bit much for a father to put on his daughter's shoulders.

Odin stared down at me over the bridge of his crooked nose. "I don't," he assured me. "You weren't supposed to exist at all."

I glared at him. "You're not making me feel any better."

He continued as if I hadn't said anything. "Freya and I were not supposed to love one another. When she became pregnant, we knew we'd pay the ultimate price for our violation." He closed his eyes. "The last time we had a child, we were thrown out of Asgard. Freya thought you could be different, but we should have known better. Where Baldr was all of our hate, you are all of our love and it crushes you with the pain that comes with that burden. Now, I fear, Ragnarök will be too strong, and the Bifrost is out of our reach while Baldr puts us on the defensive. For once, the darkness might just win."

The blood drained from my face. I knew that Baldr was my brother, but it hadn't occurred to me that my parents viewed him as their punishment. Freya had tried to suppress my tendency for love, but she'd failed. If I was all their love… then what was Baldr?

"Maybe if you'd shown my brother and me more love instead of the boundary of laws and rules, things wouldn't be like they are now."

Odin's eyes glittered with raw power. "Freya and I are the result of Immortals who've lived without boundaries. That's how Ragnarök was born in the first place." His gaze darkened. "You are our weakness. We loved you and allowed you to test those boundaries. Now the universe will pay for our failure."

I wasn't going to let Odin frighten me. "Stop being so pathetic," I snapped, and he blinked at me in surprise. "I wanted answers, and now you gave them to me. Now tell me where Will and Tyler are being held and help me bust them out. If I'm the one who set Ragnarök free, then I'm the one that's going to shove it back in its prison."

Odin faded, and I could have roared with rage as he left me alone. I stood there in silence as I wondered if my father had just abandoned me.

Then the door clicked.

LIGHT AND DARK

A faint golden trail hovered in the air and wound down Einherjar's hallways. I followed it, hoping that my father would lead me to Will and Tyler and not into one of Freya's traps. She'd shoved me in my room like a disobedient child. Even if she didn't expect me to break free, I made sure to cover myself in a sheen of darkness like I'd felt Tyler do. Ragnarök was the result of suffering and pain, something that was the flip side of the coin of love. I had plenty of that burning in my heart. Guilt. Betrayal. Need. It all gave me a dark strength that fueled my control over the space-time web, and gave me enough strength to create a ripple around me that hovered just above my skin.

Whispers accompanied the dark magic, but I ignored them now that I knew what they were. My suffering wasn't alone. I attracted the unseen bits of broken souls that filtered through the cosmos. And on a place like the Einherjar, there were a lot of lost souls hidden in the walls. The tree in the center of its core spanned the entire ship and trapped those souls here until Freya was ready to use them. My list of things to burn was growing larger, and this ship was certainly one of them.

The golden trail stopped at a lockcd door, and then another click sounded as I approached. The heavy vault lifted and revealed Will and Tyler bound in iron chains and shoved against the wall. Burn streaks spattered across the metal, telling me that Will and Tyler had not gone down without a fight.

Tyler snapped his head up at my entrance and his lips lifted in a mischievous grin. The dark void of his eyes still remained and the black runes glimmered underneath his torn leathers. "About time," he said.

Will rattled his chains. "I'm so glad you're here," he said, his words on the exhale of pure relief. "I can't take another second with this asshole. He's a hundred times worse with the creepy runes making him nuts."

Tyler glowered and his skin flashed with a dark glimmer that reminded me of the stretching fingers devouring Muspelheim. "Your girlfriend brings out the worst in me. What can I say?"

Will growled. I summoned my spear and stabbed it against the ground. "Enough!"

Both guys looked at me, their enraged expressions becoming sheepish. "Sorry," they said in unison.

My lips twitched, wanting to smile at how cute they could be. I kept my composure, trying to keep my upper hand of authority in this situation—which was pretty easy to do when I wasn't the one in chains.

I walked to Will first and he offered his wrists. "Don't move," I commanded and lashed down with my spear. Sparks flew as the chains broke under the power of my magic. Will raised a brow at me. I was getting stronger and I wasn't the only one who'd noticed.

Ignoring him, I walked over to Tyler and dismantled his chains as well. He shook them off as they withered into a pile of ash at our feet. "Impressive," he remarked and his grin widened.

I resisted the urge to take a step back when his canines extended into sharp points. "That's new," I said.

He reached up to graze his tooth and winced when he

pricked the sharp point. "Well, that certainly isn't good."

Will took my arm and pulled me away from Tyler. "I don't know what's going on with him, but I'd keep my distance if I were you." He leaned in closer to my ear and lowered his voice. "Did Freya do something to him?"

I shook my head. "This is my fault. I—" I couldn't say the rest out loud. What I wanted to say sounded too much like my father's lament—and would only hurt Will.

My love did this.

I couldn't think about what damage my love could do. I'd gotten so much stronger since I'd learned how to love. Slipping between the folds of space and time, as well as bringing Will and Tyler with me, showed how far I'd come with the power all attained through love. Perhaps the world wasn't doomed. Perhaps I could even learn how to stop Ragnarök.

The first step was to escape this ship. My skin crackled with dark magic that kept me hidden, but its weight was already making my eyelids droop. I couldn't keep this up forever, and I certainly couldn't step through the space-time web again... not without a little boost of magic. "Tyler," I said in my most commanding voice, "you need to get us back to that tree."

*W*ill voiced all his concerns with my plan—and loudly.

"Enough," I hissed. "I'm cloaking us, but Freya isn't deaf. You keep that racket up and she's going to hear us, then it's back in chains."

"Yeah," Tyler added. He gave me a wink. "Only one girl is allowed to tie me up."

Will scoffed and wedged himself securely between Tyler and me. "You're disgusting when you've gone all dark side."

Tyler's magic whispered over him in a wave and he grinned as if he was doing it on purpose. Was it actually getting stronger?

I glared at him. "If you're going to indulge him, then why don't you cloak us? I'm getting tired." I only had the one rune along my knuckles, but it was growing larger. It stretched long fingers up to my elbow and wasn't showing any signs of stopping.

He glanced at it and winced. "Aerie, that thing is reacting to me. Being around me is only making it worse."

I took Will's hand. He raised an eyebrow, but I had a theory. "I'm going to ask you a weird question. You need to answer, and honestly."

Tyler moved as if to fall back and leave Will and I alone, but I shook my head.

"You can ask me anything," Will said. The honesty in his voice bit like a viper. I didn't want to hurt him, but I needed him to remember what we had together.

I kept a tight grip on Will's hand. "Do you remember the first time we met?"

"Which time?" he asked. Now that he was a Valiant, he would remember his past lives.

I bit my lip. "The best one."

His eyelids fluttered closed and his fingers clenched around mine. "It was on a beach."

I knew that beach. Both pain and pleasure filled me through the memories bound between us. It's where we'd fallen in love in another life… and where we'd been ripped apart in the most horrible of ways.

As if I'd turned off a switch, the darkness writhing over me solidified into tiny bits of ash and drifted grains over my skin. The space-time web fluctuated, sending the walls around me bowing. Normally I would have triggered a time freeze—but now I knew what I was doing.

Instead of letting myself be dragged in by the immense weight in the space-time net fueled by my shock and sorrow, I commanded it. I reeled it in and secured it into the center of my chest where I'd always thought my flame as a Valkyrie resided. The heat wasn't because I was a Valkyrie. It was my capacity for love.

Tyler stretched out and sent a wave of darkness over us, effectively shrouding us before the ships scanners could detect our presence. "That was foolish," he remarked, but he tilted his head, looking both pensive and intrigued.

I straightened. "It was necessary." I needed Tyler to see that I was capable of controlling my darkness. With Will to bring me back and remind me about the mortal part of myself, I could undo even the weighty power of Ragnarök. There was *hope.*

"Now come on," I insisted and tugged Will with me.

He stumbled, still stunned at what had happened. "Where are we going?" he asked.

"We're going to free some souls."

———

I should have known it'd been too easy to free Will and Tyler. The moment we stepped around the bend and arrived at the glittering doors that separated us from the Einherjar's core, two scowling gods stood in our way.

I kept my grip on Will's hand. He was my anchor to the rage that bubbled up inside of me. If Odin had betrayed me just to see what I'd do, then he knew where my alliances were now.

"I expected you to choose one," Odin mused.

Freya's spear glowed with embers and the edge of its blade licked with tiny flames. It only did that when she was very angry. "I expected her to reap them both after what they made her do." She lifted her lip in a snarl. "It's because of them that you triggered Ragnarök. Why would you bring them here? Why would you defy me?" She growled and streaks of red ran down her arms and spidered out at her feet. "You break the laws of the Valkyrie over and over again as if you've learned nothing at all. I've been too easy on you."

It was the glimmer of tears in her eyes that betrayed the source of her anger.

She was afraid. Afraid of losing me—or having to put me down.

"I am not Baldr," I said through clenched teeth. "I didn't want to trigger Ragnarök."

I'd never seen Odin summon his weapon, but a great axe appeared and flattened against Freya's stomach to prevent her from lunging at me. "Calm yourself," he commanded.

Apparently, my brother's name was a trigger-word.

Freya seethed, and in that moment she was not my mother. She was the goddess of war who'd been challenged. In war, challenges needed to be removed.

Will released my hand and took a brave step, putting himself between two gods and their target. "Odin," he said. My father raised his chin and acknowledged the latest addition to his army. Will splayed out his fingers and the golden magic of his Immortality danced over his skin. "I didn't ask for this gift, but you gave it to me." His fingers clenched. "If the power of suffering souls is what keeps the Einherjar running, if the power of a soul is what will give your wife what she needs to save Muspelheim and her daughters trapped down there, then I give my own freely."

I clenched onto Will's wrist. "What're you doing?" I hissed.

Will glanced at me and gave a slight nod as if to say *Trust me.*

Freya seemed to be jolted out of her rage by the offer. The blaze of red in her eyes calmed to sizzling embers. "I lost a daughter," she said, almost numbly. "There is nothing that can be done to save her—not even your sacrifice."

I stiffened, wondering if she'd seen what was left of Sam and the undead Valkyries still trapped on Muspelheim.

"You're right," Will said. "But you have daughters down there still alive. And the souls trapped in the Einherjar's core have suffered long enough. You torment them and drain them dry." He pointed at the wall that glittered with crystal and took another step. "You don't need the souls that couldn't survive their Valkyries. You need someone who did." He opened his arms again and leaned his head back, exposing his neck. "Take what you need, and in exchange, you will set them free."

Will was right. All of those broken souls were useless trinkets compared to the burning blaze of his soul. The Valkyries had never reaped an Immortal's soul— not that I was aware of. Whereas a mortal's soul had limits... a soul like Will's had none.

Freya clenched her spear until her knuckles went white. I had a feeling that it was a motion made to restrain herself from pressing a deadly sequence of buttons. "Ragnarök is already upon us. You dare to offer me a deal?" She snarled and her eyes burned until I couldn't even recognize her anymore. "I will never give up the power that is rightfully mine. Your soul was supposed to have been ours, but you fell into Odin's service by my daughter's sacrifice. Perhaps I should just take you for punishment of what you've done."

"Mother!" I snapped and shoved Will aside. A wave of heat exploded at my shoulder blades and my wings threatened to burst through delicate mortal skin. I couldn't allow myself to lose my human form. If I embraced all the rage and fire that came with being a Valkyrie, I'd turn into the very thing I was growing to despise. "As your daughter, I am begging you to give me this chance to fix the damage I've caused." I lowered my voice. "I'm asking you to trust me."

My mother's fingers twitched and I didn't hesitate. I summoned my spear and tossed it. My aim had always been good, but landing the blow so that I broke her death-grip on her weapon without hurting her took skill—and a bit of luck.

The weapon clattered to the floor and every Immortal just stood there, stunned.

I moved fast before they could recover from their shock. I embraced the deeper part of me that fueled my Immortality and my connection to Ragnarök. Time and space warped, sending me catapulting towards the spear lying on the ground. I snatched it up and pointed it at my mother. "Stand aside."

"Daughter. You don't know how to use my weapon," Freya said. As strong as her words sounded, her voice strained until taut.

I hovered my finger over one of the buttons. I didn't know how to use it. I could just smash away at it and I had no doubt terrible things would happen. "Just get out of my way and you can have it back."

She didn't move, but her eyes glowed with embers as she watched me. "I have survived Ragnarök before only because I'd prepared for the day when it would return. Those souls are how we survive, Daughter. You cannot have them."

I growled. She wasn't looking at the bigger picture. "For once in your life, will you listen to me? After everything I've been through, I learned what it meant to deal with the darkness inside of me. I've overcome Ragnarök every single day I've been alive."

Freya flinched. "I tried to protect you from it." Her gaze fell on Tyler. "That's why I allowed the Heimdall anywhere near you."

My eyes narrowed. "Do you even understand why he stabilized me?"

She raised an eyebrow. "He holds the same darkness of Ragnarök inside of him." She glanced at Odin and gave him a slight nod of appreciation. "It is my husband who knows how to filter out the shadows."

Odin agreed with a stomp of his foot. "I discovered the power of sunlight early in my years of Immortality. It subdues Ragnarok and any echoes it might leave behind."

"No," I said, the word a final thud against my ears. Both my parents straightened at the challenge. "You've only learned how to suppress it. I have learned how to *fight* it." Tyler had helped me because he awakened friendship and hope in me. When I'd come of age and was threatened to be dragged under by the ugliness of reaping souls, it was Will's love that grounded me.

Ragnarök only knew loss. It sank into the weight of space and time created by humanity's suffering and pain. Love gone wrong could easily make that pain a hundredfold deeper... but it was also love that gave hope. There was another side to Ragnarök. I saw it every time I looked into the eyes of someone who loved me. I saw it in Will. I saw it in Tyler. I even saw its glimmer in the backs of my mother's eyes as she watched me with her breath caught in her throat. The universe was too balanced for there to only be doom and gloom.

There was love. There was Yggdrasil.

I was going to get there. If heartbreak was how I fell, then love was how I soared. Love was how I'd get to Yggdrasil and end Ragnarök's course of destruction.

"We do this my way," I said and lifted my chin. I brandished the spear at my mother. "You've run from

Ragnarök for too long. It's time that the cycle is ended."

Freya hesitated, then looked to Odin for guidance.

My father lowered his weapon and frowned. "We've tried it our way," he said after a long moment of silence. "Perhaps we should humble ourselves and give our child a chance to do what we never could."

Freya's brows drew together as if she were pained by his response. "But what if she fails?" Her voice broke on the last word. A Valkyrie's failure against Ragnarök meant the end of the universe itself. "There will be nothing left."

Odin shook his head and his weapon vanished in a flash of light. He took Freya's chin in a gentle pinch as he leaned in. "You know that's not true. We've watched Ragnarök destroy the universe over and over again. We hide like cowards until it has devoured every last atom. We rebuild what's left and start anew." For the first time, the glimmer of sunlight in his eyes dimmed. "I'm tired of starting over."

Freya didn't look convinced, but she allowed him to pull her out of the way so that the crystal door to the Einherjar's core was free. I edged around them and pressed against its sharp edges, but it wouldn't open for me. I looked at Tyler and he understood my unspoken need. He rested a hand against the wall, and I paid attention to what he didn't this time. He drew on the suffering of darkness inside himself, and that's what the Einherjar reacted to.

My stomach churned and nausea threatened to overcome me. This was how I knew that the Einherjar had perverted the basis of Yggdrasil. A true resting place for souls wouldn't be capable of recognizing suffering, but the core rumbled at the hint of it as shadows spiraled around Tyler's fingers. Suffering was all it ever knew.

The door hissed open and I followed Tyler inside with new resolve.

I was going to do exactly what Ragnarök did every time it demolished the universe, except this time, I wouldn't leave only suffering behind. I'd take it all away until only raw, innocent humanity was left.

TRUST

Once inside Einherjar's core, souls whipped in panic at the sight of Freya's spear still in my grip. I leaned it against the wall, trusting that my mother wouldn't come rushing in after it. I suspected that if she really hadn't wanted me to enter Einherjar's core, she would have stopped me—spear or not.

Will followed us inside and the door hissed closed, leaving me with a sense of entrapment. The power and suffering in this place weighed the space-time web harsher than anything I'd ever felt. Now that I knew what to look for, I sensed the mass that could call Ragnarök through worlds. It was no wonder Muspelheim had been its first target. The Einherjar held all the souls that Valkyries had reaped... but it was Muspelheim that held the grave of a thousand dead Valkyries that had devoured those very souls at their birth and lived with the guilt and suffering of their duty every day.

I shifted closer to the winding roots that formed the base of the long tree that soared through the center of the ship. Blue spirits glittered around it and sang their low lament, settling down now that I'd released my weapon.

Will's fingers wound around mine as Tyler pressed a hand against one of the roots that arched high above his head. He scratched at the bark, revealing oily grime that flaked away to reveal the wires buried underneath. The ship itself fed off of these souls and I shivered.

"Shine bright," I said through the pain that clenched around my chest.

Will blinked at me. "What?"

I held his grip tighter. "Burn hot with the power of Odin. Take away their pain."

I'd seen Tyler do it over and over again. He seared away the darkness with the power of sunlight. It wasn't love, but it burned hot like love and kept the icy chill at bay. I could do that for these souls... and maybe it'd be enough to set them free.

Tyler came to my side in an instant, his eyes the crystal worry of one of the Valiant who only wanted to protect. "Are you sure?"

I nodded and stiffened my lower lip to prevent the tears that threatened to spill over my cheeks. "I need to do this. Don't worry. I will survive."

Tyler offered his hand. "You'd better."

With my left grip on Will, I gave my free hand to Tyler and drew him to my side.

I'd never felt more loved and protected than I did right then with both Valiant warriors opening their hearts and their love to me. They were two halves of my heart and I was just a husk without them.

I closed my eyes and nodded. "I'm ready."

They hesitated, but then the heat came. It grew in low, rolling waves like thunder of a storm. Then it seared against me, running up my fingertips to my elbows until the fiery fingers threatened to disintegrate me from the inside.

I opened my heart to the pain and the souls gave a high-pitched trill in recognition as they penetrated my chest and curled up in the open space of my soul where the echoes of Ragnarök lived.

I was the conduit. I was the weight in the space-time web that would draw them in…

and it was my Valiant who would set them free.

The scent of sunlight and embers embraced me… and then I died.

YGGDRASIL

Death. But only a temporary death. This was the glimpse of Yggdrasil I needed to capture a weapon against Ragnarök and its never-ending hunger.

I opened my eyes, but regretted it the moment I did. The impact of purity and love soared into the heavens in the form of a great, golden tree that exuded not sunlight, but pure and unadulterated love and joy. It gleamed with radiance and souls free of suffering and pain danced through its leaves, sharing all they'd learned in their journey to earth.

Crystal blooms budded under its leaves, reminding me of Odin's gifts. He'd harnessed sunlight, but that crystal is what I saw in a Valiant's eyes. Perhaps mother wasn't the only Immortal who hid behind her

title of god of war. There was a heart in there somewhere, even if it was one encased by steel.

A yearning lifted my spirit up, threatening to tear me
from my body so that I could join the souls dancing
through Yggdrasil's branches. How I wanted to. This
felt like home. This was a place where I'd never
know pain.

Two strong hands held mine on the mortal plane
where space and time threaded together in an overlap-
ping tapestry.

Will.

Tyler.

I couldn't leave them to Ragnarök and the jaws of its
dark fate.

I forced my eyes to roam lower among the branches
that glittered with blooms until I got to the low-
hanging fruit of souls full of the golden weight of
Yggdrasil's sap. A minuscule breeze sang through the
limbs, sending the crystal leaves clinking against one
another in a beautiful symphony.

The largest of the golden fruits broke free... and
dropped.

I dove for it. If that fruit made it into the space-time web, it would become a soul with a mind and a life and a conscience. It'd have a purpose... but I had greater plans in mind.

I snatched the fruit up and the tree groaned as if it'd just noticed the disturbance. The low mist at the base covered the thin layer of soil that separated this realm from that of my own.

"I'm sorry," I whispered and my voice disappeared into the weightlessness of an afterlife I'd never get to see again.

*T*he warmth of Yggdrasil retreated, leaving me with an icy chill that settled over my bones and made my teeth chatter so hard I was sure I was going to dislocate my jaw.

"Tyler," I cried, the name coming to me unbidden as familiar pain wrapped spiked claws around my body. This is what it felt like when I was ripped from the promise of love and hope, only to find myself immersed in darkness.

Time and space vibrated around me like a weeping

thing trapped in sobs. Needles pricked against my skin as my limbs fell asleep against the cold that struggled to reach inside until it grazed my soul. My stomach dropped and my hands shot out looking for something to grab onto as the sensation of falling made me panic.

Tyler's strong arms wrapped around me and I curled into his chest and his warmth, the helpless sensation immediately easing under the undeniable promise of his strength. I pressed my entire body as close to his as I could as I greedily drew in his heat. Memories unlocked with a soft *snap* as another box opened, filling me with all the times Tyler had done this for me before. He stroked my hair and shushed me as he pulled the darkness out of me… and into himself.

I cringed when I realized this was why my mother had allowed him anywhere near me. Something had to give when I tampered with space and time. I'd learned the price of opening my heart to it and attracting the weight of sorrow that existed in the echoes of Ragnarök. That price was Tyler's suffering, as well as my own.

Torment clawed at me and I found the strength to try and pull away, but Tyler's arms were solid iron and wrapped around me like prison bars. "You're not going anywhere," he chided in a hushed whisper. "You pushed yourself too far."

I knew he was right. The other times I'd used my gifts to this extent had been accidental—but my trip to Yggdrasil was beyond anything I'd ever attempted before.

That's when I remembered the hum of heat I still clutched in my hands at my chest.

I wriggled in Tyler's grasp and looked down as I forced my frozen fingers to open.

A golden fruit with the purest light of life emanating from its core gleamed back at me.

"What is that?" Will breathed.

I'd almost forgotten that Will was still with us, and that we were in Einherjar's core with a tumult of souls still whipping around us… but there was less of them. I craned my neck up to peer at the small gathering of blue dots that twinkled like stars. I hadn't managed to save all of the souls, but at least I'd helped some of them escape this place.

When I looked back at Tyler… he would not meet my gaze.

DEGRADATION

 reya wouldn't face us for the rest of the evening. Even though there was no sun to guide our days, and only a perpetual darkness that clouded my homeworld of Muspelheim, the ship continued its cycle of natural lights that lined the walls. It dimmed into the soft hue of evening and my stomach growled for dinner.

Even though my body was starving after expending so much energy, nausea prevented me from even the contemplation of eating food.

I'd settled for a warm bowl of soup which a Valkyrie had placed in front of me. We'd come to the mess hall which was small in comparison to a ship of this size. A handful of tables boasted the few Valkyries who still had their mortal form, having returned from reaping their souls. Their skin was pale and their lustrous hair turned scraggly as it hung about their chest in clumps.

"What's wrong with them?" Will asked.

Tyler had gone with Odin and Freya to "discuss matters," whatever that meant. I'd refused to part with my magical fruit and it rested on the inside of my jacket, out of sight, but it continued to hum its other-worldly song against the wall of my chest. The other Valkyries seemed to sense its healing power and glanced at me, nervously looking away when I caught their gaze.

"They're shedding their mortal bodies." I swirled my spoon in the contents of my soup that'd long gone cold.

A Valkyrie assigned with making sure I finished at least a few bites by Freya herself walked to us and frowned. Her wings draped over her shoulders in slow, drifting waves. "You're not eating," she observed.

I glowered at her. My stomach couldn't possibly process food. "It's cold," I complained.

Her shoulders relaxed. "Oh, is that all?" She reached over Will as if she'd forgotten he was there and he leaned to keep from getting an elbow in his face.

Embers fluttered to life at her fingertips and then a flame appeared. She gripped the bowl, sending the contents frothing with heat before she released it. "There," she said, satisfied with her handiwork. "Now make sure you eat up. Freya is not in a good mood."

"When is she ever?" I growled.

The Valkyrie smirked. "Hang in there, Val. We're all just trying to get through this one step at a time." She bowed, then her wings fluttered before she left.

"What was that about?" Will asked as he leaned closer. "Do you know her?"

I tried to watch the Valkyrie as she sauntered away, her gait majestic and graceful as was native to the race... except when it came to me. Her wings, black as midnight, shimmered and looked beautiful even against the ship's harsh lights. "No," I finally admitted. My memories of the Einherjar were fragmented at best. I'd been trying so hard to reclaim my life on Earth that I'd let so many things about my Immortal life slip away. She was just one of many Valkyries to me now. Their perfection and poise blended together until they were nothing but a pristine race that represented my torment and my imprisonment to an old way of life.

Then my gaze went back to the Valkyries still struggling to eat. The one who'd helped me found a few more with cold soup and set their bowls warming with her touch. They smiled their thanks, but their eyes were tired and their shoulders hunched as if already feeling the weight of their wings.

"You said they're shedding their mortal bodies," Will said, lowering his voice so that only I could hear him. He eyed my bowl of soup, seeming to concentrate on it far harder than he needed to. "Does that mean you're going to lose your body too?"

I startled and dropped my spoon. It clattered to the table and Will picked it up, wiping it off with my napkin before offering it back to me. I stared at the twisted metal that reflected my human face. Every Valkyrie was linked to her soul, and when Will died, the deterioration should have begun. I'd been clinging to my mortal body with such ferocity that I'd almost forgotten I wasn't supposed to have it at all.

He lowered the spoon back to the table and wrapped his fingers around mine. I hadn't realized that I'd started shaking. I met his gaze, suddenly feeling frantic as fear gripped my heart. I couldn't save the world, I couldn't save him, and what if I couldn't even save myself?

"Val," he whispered, bringing me back to the present just as he always did, "you're doing it again."

"What?" I asked and my voice shook.

He grinned and his thumb stroked over my knuckles. "You're spiraling and trying to hold the universe on your shoulders. You're really good at that."

He drew me in and I allowed myself to curl into the curve of his chest where I fit perfectly. He stroked my hair and we watched the other Valkyries go about the mess hall until the lights eventually dimmed and we were the only ones left.

"Do you think it's because of the rune on your hand?" he asked.

I hadn't realized that he'd been stroking the black mark that continued to grow. I knew what it was now. It was the same darkness that ran in the Heimdall line and the same power that had made my parents Immortal—and spawned Ragnarök. "Is it a bad thing to hold onto my mortality?" I asked. Even though I felt my mortality acutely in this body—the hunger, the fatigue—I didn't want to let it go. Resting against Will's chest reminded me why I'd fallen in love with him. It was this very moment. Sitting together, *being* together, even when the world around us was falling apart and death loomed around the corner. This was part of what it meant to be mortal and it made the moment even more precious. I peered up at Will, unable to resist the urge to run a finger across the perfect arch of his cheek. "Is it wrong to hope you can get yours back?"

He winced as if I'd stung him and I pulled away, realizing that I'd summoned an ember and burned him. "I'm sorry," I murmured. Even though I was still a Valkyrie, he was a Valiant. I shouldn't have the ability to burn him.

The warmth radiating across my chest wasn't just my feelings for him. It was the power of the stolen fruit I'd taken from Yggdrasil. I pulled it out and its golden glow cascaded across the table as if its light was a tangible substance set free into the world. It drifted and rolled until it reached the floor, then finally dissipated in a fog of glitter.

"What do you plan on doing with that?" he asked. He ran his fingers around mine, but didn't venture near the fruit's flesh.

"I believe there are two possibilities this fruit can offer." I turned it in my hand and marveled at the golden glitter. "I could stop Ragnarök…"

Will leaned his cheek against my head. "Or?"

I folded the fruit into my jacket, dousing us in the gentle darkness of the sleepy mess hall.

"Or, I could save you."

---

*W*ill tried to assure me that there was nothing to save him *from*, but I'd seen the glimmer of hope in his eyes. He didn't want this life as an Immortal. He wanted to go back home and live a life he'd been denied multiple times over.

I wanted that for Will. I wanted him to live a full life and then return to Yggdrasil with all the wondrous things he'd experienced. With the power of the stolen fruit, perhaps that vision was within my reach… if only Ragnarök wasn't devouring the universe.

No matter how I looked at it, Ragnarök had to be stopped first, and I certainly wasn't strong enough to stop it on my own.

Somehow I'd fallen asleep after Will had guided me back to my room. I barely remembered him laying me down on the plush bed. Blankets stuffed with Valkyrie feathers coddled me in comforting warmth until sleep overwhelmed me. I dreamed of Yggdrasil and the souls that slipped freely through her leaves. It could have been the best dream I'd ever had in my life—except for the fact that Ragnarök itself woke me up.

A crash buckled the ship, sending it pitching and toppling me off the bed. The gravity wells lurched trying to compensate and slammed me back the other way.

Bruises blossomed across my arms as I blocked a wave of crumpled furniture tumbling right onto my head.

Will's voice shouted, muffled by the chaos that surrounded us, but I couldn't even release a scream. I put all my energy into grating my bones against the heavy iron that threatened to flatten me into the ship's hull.

Yggdrasil's promising warmth radiated against my chest, tempting me to use the power to save myself. I ground my teeth against the fleeting thought. Even if something happened to me, the fruit could still be used to stop Ragnarök. I couldn't be so selfish to save myself, only to doom the universe to certain death.

The next thought that slipped into my mind was of the swollen darkness that festered in my soul. If I wouldn't use the light… perhaps I should use the dark.

My bones crunched as I failed to hold up against the weight of the bedroom furniture bearing down on me. Of course Freya had to garnish the room with weighted weapon cases, likely filled to the brim. Devices meant to protect us were about to crush the life out of me.

Another rumble shook the ship and the sound of metal on metal rang against my ears. Will slashed away at the bulky object and continued to shout, but he wasn't going to get to me in time.

I closed my eyes and took a deep breath as I tried to escape the deep ache that ran through my arms. Slicing pain jabbed as the weight crushed me just a little bit more and my mortal body strained to hold up against a losing battle.

The darkness offered reprieve against the pain. I also knew that accepting the darkness was a step towards Tyler, towards Ragnarök and a future that couldn't possibly have a good ending. But dying right now would mean Ragnarok won all the same. I felt its icy claws wrapping around Muspelheim and reaching for the ship. Its disturbance against space and time rattled the ship's sensors and threatened to pull us under an invisible well from which there was no return.

A sound escaped me, and I realized it was a cry of frustration. I was so tired of losing. I was sick of Ragnarök and the constant threat looming over my head.

I was sick of love tearing me apart.

A rip sounded across my back as my Valkyrie wings burst through and I groaned against the wave of pain. There was a reason Valkyries shed their mortal bodies slowly in the form of a slow degradation until the flesh peeled away like old skin. The transition from mortality and a biological form designed for a beginning and an end couldn't be something less than subtle. To adopt something so foreign as Immortality and the fiery, Immortal body that came with it meant shredding yourself apart from the inside out. The pain could be enough to make someone go mad.

I'd shed my Immortal skin before on my trip from Muspelheim, and while that'd been rough, it was nothing like this. I embraced the powers inside of me, the Immortality, the flames, and most of all, the darkness that fueled my deepest skills over space and time. It should have been a gradual reacceptance of the things I'd forgotten, but my Immortality came crashing into me with the force of a thousand blades and a burn so raw, it was as if I'd been set aflame.

My wings stretched and flames engulfed my back, sending my beloved jacket disintegrating into ash that tricked down my arms. I caught Yggdrasil's fruit before it fell and wasn't surprised my flames couldn't even mar its glory.

My transformation didn't slow even with the power of Yggdrasil in my grasp. My shadows swirled and writhed across my arms and bound my wrists like chains. The once heavy furniture toppled to the side as I shrugged it away, only to reveal a shocked Valiant staring me down with a blade dulled against the onslaught he'd given my bedroom.

The ship continued to pitch, but my legs moved with it and my wings fanned out to give me balance. My world tinted in red as the flames of Muspelheim awakened in my heart. The pain ebbed and delight rushed in to take its place. How could I have fought this? Why would I have denied myself my true form? Power surged down my arms and my world lit up with a thousand lights as I drew on my external senses that caught the ebb and flow of the stars, of space and of time.

"Once again, you show me I'm not worthy." Will dropped to one knee and bowed his head. "You truly are a goddess."

If I hadn't quite literally been on fire, I would have felt the blush that crept over my face. Here I was, completely topless, being called a goddess. "Don't be so dramatic," I muttered as I rummaged through the remains of the room. One closet built into the wall held a small bounty of Valkyrie vests and I wrapped one around, tucking it tightly against my protesting wings until they squeezed through.

I turned to find Will watching me. His gaze averted. "Sorry. It's just, you're…"

I rolled my eyes. "Yes, a Valkyrie." I gripped his arm and yanked him to his feet. "There's no time for that," I assured him, even though my voice came out musical and strange to my ears. I rushed to the window and searched the darkness for any sign of our attackers. "Do you see them?"

He shook his head. "Nothing."

Flames lit the backs of my eyes and seared my irises, warping my senses until I spotted the heat signatures… or lack thereof.

A cold, terrifying void wrapped around the volcanic planet. The Einherjar could have been raining flames down onto it, but that wouldn't have done much good. This wasn't an enemy we could fight with weapons…

but the onslaught that disrupted our gravity wells didn't have such strength.

A sprinkle of ships descended on us and disappeared beneath my window, going under and around the ship. Tiny arms extended and gripped against the hull. Lights flashed, followed by zaps as the enemy worked to drill its way in. Air hissed and alarms blared. They'd breached the hull all over the ship.

Tucking Yggdrasil's fruit into a secure pouch at my hip, I grabbed Will by the arm. "Come on. We're going to the bridge."

UNDER SIEGE

*J*f I'd still been human, there was no way we could have gotten to the bridge. Freya and Odin effortlessly bypassed the light-speed airlocks, going to and from secure areas as they pleased. As a Valkyrie, it was tough, but I could do it. I pinned my wings close to my back and concentrated on the blips of space-time before each door before ripping it open and dragging Will through with me.

By the time we got to the open room that glittered with crystals and hologram stars, two gods glowered down at me, followed by Tyler who was decked out with what I could only describe as a crystal suit.

"What on Earth are you wearing?" I asked and curled my lip. Rainbow was so not his color.

He gave me a raised brow. "I could ask you the same."

Even though his mood was somber, I sensed the excitement in his tone. I'd embraced my Valkyrie… I'd embraced the darkness that brought me one step closer to him.

"This is no Earth," Freya snapped. She pointed the spear at me, but her fingers stayed clear of its buttons. "Tyler has agreed to take care of our Skuld problem." She rested the butt of her spear on the ground. "Why didn't you tell me you wanted to shed your mortal form? I could have eased your transition."

Will growled and stepped in front of me. "She nearly died. She was forced to transform. This ship of yours is a deathtrap."

To anyone else, Freya would have seemed unmoved by the statement. Her finger on her spear twitched, a sure sign that she was reigning in emotion she wasn't supposed to be feeling. "My daughters can take care of themselves, most of all Valerie."

I wasn't interested in a debate of my capability, or everyone's thoughts that I'd sprouted wings and flames mixed with shadow at my feet. I was supposed to be a creature of fire, but I was something else, too. My parents had rejected the darkness until it created Ragnarök. I wouldn't make that same mistake. I'd deal with my pain instead of trying to bury it in another dimension.

"How is Tyler going to help you?" I asked.

Tyler proceeded to ignore me as he climbed into a glass tube.

I'd seen other supernatural creatures use it before—or rather, be used by it. A space-time actuator compressed and expanded the power placed within it, and when it hummed to life, I knew I wasn't going to like whatever Tyler had planned. By the look of approval on Freya and Odin's faces, it wasn't anything good.

Odin stopped me when I moved to unlatch the actuator. "He's already begun. You are Yggdrasil's chosen and Tyler is doing this so that you may have a chance."

I frowned, but my hand absently moved to my pouch where I'd secured Yggdrasil's fruit. Freya's ember eyes followed my movements and she frowned. "Don't think I don't know what you've taken from Yggdrasil. Don't bring out that blasphemy here."

I balked at her. My mother, of all creatures, couldn't lecture me on morality. "I won't," I snapped. "I'm saving this for Ragnarök to clean up *your* mess."

She opened her mouth to retort, her knuckles white as she gripped her spear, but Tyler slammed his fists against the crystal barrier of his cage. "Enough," he snapped. His armor cracked all over and a piercing hum made me grip my ears. Light billowed from him, bled over his eyes, and Tyler embraced the one thing he hated the most: the suppression of Odin's gift to his Valiant. Only Will was strong enough not to flinch away when the Einherjar drew on Tyler's offering.

Space and time buckled around us like a web. The drilling and groans of the ship ceased against the invasion of the Skuld trying to get inside. It wasn't because Tyler had done anything to protect the ship… he'd stopped time.

As a Frigg, I could walk through manufactured bubbles of space-time. Tyler's light continued to engulf the room, and for the first time, he was able to join me in the stolen moment.

"Take Will to Muspelheim," he ordered. "My mother has betrayed us. If you can reach the Bifrost, you can stop Baldr and you can reach Ragnarök's core."

I strained to look at him through the filter of my fingers. My wings wafted behind me and my Immortal form did little to protect me from the power of Tyler's onslaught as he expanded the breach in space-time to engulf the entirety of the ship and out into space. I watched as the rainbow hue, like the edge of an Earthly soap bubble, swept through the void and wrapped around Muspelheim itself, stopping Ragnarök in its tracks. The power to hold this shouldn't have been possible. What strength was Tyler drawing from?

"What'll happen to you?" I asked, shouting over the frozen hum. Sound shouldn't have been able to travel, but this wasn't a frozen pocket of time. This was a new layer in the universe that Tyler had dragged us to, one where we moved freely and the space in our immediate vicinity reacted, but out in the distance the world had stopped spinning and the universe had been put on pause.

"I'll hold this as long as I need to," he said as he pressed his fists against the barrier. His armor gleamed and shadows licked through the cracks of his armor. "You're our only hope, Aerie. Do what must be done."

I bit my lip and wanted to tell him that this wasn't right. Whatever he was doing required nothing short of sacrifice... multiple sacrifices. Those souls I'd seen vanish from the Einherjar's core... I'd thought that they'd found peace in Yggdrasil.

I was wrong.

I looked past my bias and my love to see Tyler for what he really was. He glowed with the tell-tale sign of souls, the sickly gold that dripped from his fingers and bled through his eyes.

He was a devourer of souls.

FOLLOW ME

*P*ain mixed with grief and incomprehension. How could Tyler be even worse than my mother? She'd used souls to create her daughters and as much as I hated her for that, her actions came out of a desperate need. Ragnarök always came back. Without her daughters, without her army, it would wipe through the universe in a split second. It'd been attracted to Muspelheim and it'd stayed long enough for us to plan a course of action.

I ripped open space and time and grabbed Will's hand. Tyler gave me a final nod before I stepped through and dragged my Valiant soul with me.

Perhaps he had no choice either. He was a Heimdall, part of a line consumed by the weight of pain and suffering. If he didn't feed on souls, what would happen to him?

There were so many questions that needed answers. Answers that I couldn't hear from Tyler right now. That left only one other person... Dalia, the goddess of the Bifrost.

Stepping through a void, my stomach dropped and disorientation nearly overwhelmed me, but I kept a tight hold on Will as I concentrated on holding the portal open. The Einherjar couldn't move, not while under Tyler's spacial distortion control. When I looked back and moved my freckled feathers out of the way, I saw his light gleaming like a beacon at the end of the tunnel. I whispered prayers that he'd be okay.

The lurching portal ended and I stepped onto the hot, ashy ground of Muspelheim. This time I'd brought us to the outskirts of the city. Golden spires broke the sky and distant volcanoes made the perfect backdrop to what had once been my home.

Will stepped out behind me, his body blurring as time and space fought the foreign entity. A flash brought my attention to the sky and then a sonic boom swept the clouds sprawling until I could see the glimmering blip that was the Einherjar. A thousand glittering black dots closed in around it and my heart thudded against my chest. He'd helped me break free of the Skuld and their hold on the ship, but now I had to hope that the Valkyries and my mother, as well as my father, could keep him safe.

"He can take care of himself." Will squeezed my hand that was still holding onto his like my life depended on it. "Tyler is the strongest person I know, aside from you, of course," Will said, surprising me with his honesty.

"Yeah," I said. "It'll take more than a couple of Skuld and the echoes of Ragnarök to slow him down.

Will's eyes roamed my body, clearly getting distracted. "You're beautiful."

I rolled my eyes. "Glad to know that becoming Immortal didn't dampen your teenage hormones." I tugged him to the outskirts of the city. We called it the Jewel, the one place on Muspelheim where we could find luxury and comfort. It was a jewel indeed, a glimmering indulgence surrounding by the claws of reality that held the stone in place. Towards the outskirts resided the barracks that blended with the red hue of the landscape... and then there were the natives.

Tyler had told me to find Mr. Jefferson. I'd nearly forgotten the Jotun and collective of natives that were a natural part of the volcanic world. Like the Huldra communed with the forest, the Jotun communed with flame.

My wings twitched as we walked and I stretched them, allowing myself to adjust to their slight weight and how they changed my balance. I finally released Will's hand to give myself some space. He matched my pace as we kicked up dust and marched to the caves where I'd find the Surtr, the fire-born race of the Jotun.

"You seem content to have your Valkyrie form back," Will observed.

I curled my fingers into my palms and instinctively squeezed my wings to my shoulders. There was magic in this form and it wasn't entirely biological. The appendages would have been massively heavy if a human had somehow found a way to sprout wings. An invisible force brushed through my feathers and lit up my nerve endings with the power of the Valkyrie. I frowned, because I knew where that power came from now. How many souls had been destroyed to give me this body? "Just because I like it doesn't mean I have a right to it."

Will fell into pensive silence as we continued to walk. Then he looked up and surveyed the lazy dunes. "Why is it so quiet?"

I didn't turn back to look at the scar across the sky. "Baldr has sent his forces against the Einherjar. He believes he's already claimed Muspelheim." I shuddered when I thought of the undead Valkyrie that still roamed this planet. I had no desire to come across Sam again and the empty shell she'd become. "I don't know where the risen Valkyries will be. We should keep our eyes open."

He nodded and light flickered at his fingertips. If any trouble came our way, his sword would be ready to take care of the problem. "So where are we going?" He glanced over his shoulder. "I saw a city that way."

"Some of my sisters might still be there hiding out and waiting for Freya's orders." We'd been given countless training sessions on what to do if Muspelheim was ever under attack. The city had a maze of underground tunnels and they all led to our allies who had their own residence a few miles out. "If they're smart, they'll follow protocol."

We continued the long trek. I couldn't have directed the way out loud, but my muscle memory kicked in and knew exactly where to go. Freya had dropped us all over the planet and told us to find the caves. It sometimes took weeks, but as an Immortal I didn't need food. Rest and nourishment were only luxuries.

Luckily this trek wasn't a long one. After two hours, and two stops to hide from drifting black clouds that represented the patrolling Skuld still left on the planet, I spotted the divots in the red clay and ash that meant doorways to the caves.

I flared my wings and vaulted to one, looking back at Will when he made a sound of surprise. He laughed. "Sorry. I just forget that those wings aren't just for show. You really know how to use them."

I tucked them to my back again, wishing it wasn't so easy to slip back into my natural form. I recognized the way Will looked at me. It was the same way I'd viewed him when he'd changed from his human form to the perfect hard edges of one of the Valiant. He'd seemed too perfect, something I couldn't touch and kept lifted on a pedestal. "Once this is all over, I'm going to figure out how to get my mortal body back. You don't have to look at me like I'm something majestic."

He swept fingers over my feathers, the caress making

me tremble. The nerve endings along the supernatural appendages were incredibly sensitive, designed to help me sense shifts in the air. "But you are majestic," he insisted. "Why would you want to be human again?"

I frowned and pulled away. "The same reason you want to be human again, I imagine."

Guilt swept over his features, his brows drawing together and his fingers folding into fists. "That's different. I see how you look at me like I'm something to be pitied. This body only makes you think of Tyler and he does such a better job at being an Immortal than I do."

I hadn't even thought that Will might compare himself to Tyler in that way. I knelt and swept away the ash, revealing a hatch with rusted hinges. I lifted, and what would have been impossibly heavy for me in my human form was a featherlight motion for a Valkyrie. There was some benefit to losing my mortal body, at least.

A draft of cool air burst through the tunnel and swept my hair from my face. I fluttered my eyes closed at the refreshing breeze. Cleaner drones filtered the air and fluttered through the darkness like fireflies. Keeping my wings close to my back, I slipped inside.

Will dropped down beside me, then looked up at the square hole we'd come through. "How are we going to close the hatch?"

Waving him away, I found a panel and popped it open. Grateful for my memories finally returning, I plugged in the code to electronically close the hatch. A fan sounded as it worked to reorient the ash over the hatch and keep it hidden from view.

Will nodded, his eyes a dim glow as his Valiant form fought against the darkness. "Impressive."

I allowed my vision to adjust to the long hall that led through the maze of caves. Once inside, the network could be a trap if one didn't know where to go. The Surtr were adept at mimicking the way volcanoes worked, sprouting roots as the lava fought to escape its chamber. Except this time I didn't want to escape; I wanted to find the molten core.

Will took a few steps and paused at the first intersection. Both tunnels looked exactly the same. Lights flickered as the cleaner drones continued their business of purifying the air, gathering near the hatch to expel the contaminants we'd brought inside. A few flickered around my wings and I vibrated my feathers, flinging them off.

Will turned and gave me a raised brow. "You got us this far. Do you remember the way?"

I searched through the array of boxes in my mind, both open and closed, and ground my teeth together. Unfortunately, none of this was ringing a bell.

While straightening and trying to look confident, I picked a tunnel at random. "This way."

---

*A*fter about an hour Will started to ask questions. "Are you sure we're going the right way."

I fluttered my wings, noting the shift in air currents that could have been a sign of an open cavern that would take us to the Surtr city, or it could have just been a swarm of cleaner drones doubling back and picking off the lasting particles of the outside world from our path.

I took another turn, following the hint, then jerked to a halt when I spotted one of the Surtr traps. If I hadn't been looking for it, I would have walked right across the spot across the floor that lit up against my thermal senses. Paper-thin tiles would give way to a vault of lava burning from underneath. A Valkyrie perhaps could survive the heat, but I wasn't going to test that theory.

When Will sighed in frustration and moved to step around me, I grabbed him by the arm just in time. His feet grazed the trap and molten heat swept up and engulfed the room. I flared my wings as much as the constricting tunnel would allow and vaulted us out of harm's way.

When he gave me an incredulous look, I released him and sighed. "Okay, fine. I have no idea where we are."

Instead of yelling at me, he smirked. "I figured as much in the first five minutes when you took us in a complete circle."

I bit my lip. I'd hoped that he hadn't noticed that. "Right." Dropping to the ground, my wings brushed around my shoulders like a cloak and I put my head between my knees. "Everyone thinks I'm some kind of champion. The fate of the universe resting in my hands is kind of a stress trigger."

He laughed and unfolded my fingers, stroking across my palms with his thumbs. The skin glittered against his touch, my Immortal form hardened and metallic, but against his Valiant marble, we made a good pair. "You're not responsible for any of this," he said.

I gazed into his eyes and saw what I always did, my reflection that countered his statement. I could have saved him had I been stronger, wiser, more capable. Instead he was trapped just as much as I was. "Do you believe in fate?"

He cocked his head. "That we're all destined for a purpose?"

I nodded. "My mother wasn't supposed to have me, but she did. Then she wasn't supposed to love me, but she did." I stroked his face. "Then I found you, and I wasn't supposed to love you, but I did. What if my fate is just an echo of my mother's failures?" She'd created Ragnarök and doomed the universe to the cycle of life and death. I didn't want to speak aloud that I felt like it was my fate to undo her mistakes. That was far too much pressure, but it was starting to weigh on me until I thought I might be crushed by the responsibility.

He smiled, encouraging and calm as always. "There's this memory I have of us together. You were always so worried about what was expected of you and the future." He swept a strand of hair behind my ear.

"Even as a powerful Frigg, you can't control the future, and trying to will only eat you up from the inside."

My heart swelled at the drifting memories. My gaze went distant as I remembered how his touch on my face felt just like it did right now. Reassuring and solid. "You told me I should live in the present." My gaze went back to his and I tried to look past the rainbow glitter of his Immortal irises. Beneath the magic was a boy with chestnut eyes with a gaze that could hold me captive and quite literally stop time. I huffed a laugh when I realized the irony. "Did I ever tell you that when I was human and I'd forgotten our history, you triggered my Frigg powers? I would stop time when you looked at me like you are now."

He leaned closer. "Even if I couldn't remember, something in me remembered you." His lips brushed mine and warmth in me stirred. "You've always been my light against the darkness."

My heart broke to hear the adoration in his voice. The raw honesty told me everything I needed to know about my relationship with Will. An unexplainable force drew us together. There wasn't anything forbidden or dangerous about it, no matter what kind of rules my mother had put in place for the Valkyries. Without him, I was lost in darkness. With him, he reminded me why life was worth living, not to focus on timelines I couldn't control. As a Frigg, I focused far too much on the timeline. I searched and prodded space and time in my desperate attempt to make the world a better place. I kissed him again, taking his advice and living in the here and now. No matter what the next five seconds, five minutes, or even five years brought me, it couldn't take this away.

JOTUNHEIM

*A*flicker of light caught our attention and we broke from the kiss that made me feel whole again. I turned to find a Surtr glowering down at us. The lengthy creature was what some might call a Minotaur, complete with bullhorns and red skin. But this Surtr wasn't going to chase us through the tunnels and eat us for dinner. I broke out into a smile and jumped into his arms. "Billy!"

Billy was around my age—a little over a hundred, and had been one of the first Surtr I'd ever met. He hugged me in return. "Our little Aerie returns to us."

He grinned, giving me a full view of serrated lines of teeth layered like a shark's. Will gripped my arm and protectively pulled me away.

I laughed. "It's fine. Billy, this is Will."

Billy eyed the human turned Valiant and sniffed. I never knew what the Surtr smelled us for, but he only seemed to tense after getting a good whiff. "Reeks of guilt."

I rolled my eyes. "He does not." I smiled and went to nudge Will, but his features had darkened.

"It's nice to meet you too," Will said, not sounding the least bit amused. He extended a hand and cleared his throat. "If you're a friend of Val's, then you're a friend of mine."

Billy gave him a slow nod of appreciation. "Come. You two have triggered enough of our traps."

Will gave me a raised brow. "What else did we trigger besides the lava pit of doom?"

I grimaced. There'd been a few spring-loaded walls that could have been triggered had I not spotted the stains on the ground. Muspelheim was under constant attack by Baldr's forces, and even though it'd never been anything strong enough to unseat my sisters from the city itself, we'd always had to deal with the Skuld and those they possessed. I shivered.

Billy narrowed his eyes. "Enough to alert us that we were either in trouble, or there was a hapless Valkyrie

wandering around with half her memories on freeze."
He motioned for us to follow. "Looks like it was
both. C'mon."

Will stuck close to my side as we trailed behind the
Surtr who clomped his way through the halls. He
seamlessly chose corridors and hit invisible buttons as
we made our way through the maze. Tunnels shifted
behind us, ensuring that even if we were being
followed, a pursuer would have a heck of a time
keeping up. They'd have to stay right on our heels.

"How do you know this creature?" Will growled.

He didn't trust the Surtr, and I didn't blame him. The
race did kind of look like something out of nightmares
in their natural form, but I'd grown up with them.
Those parts of my memories were fluttering to life,
making me dizzy as boxes unlatched in my mind and
filled me with a life before Earth, before Will and
before my duties as a Valkyrie had taken away an
otherwise pleasant childhood. Where my sisters had
been kept at a distance, it was Billy who'd been a
companion. I hadn't been around him as much as
Tyler, but Billy was the one who'd taught me the
tunnels and the way of flame. It was a near cult-like
fascination the Surtr had with Muspelheim's core.

My nose crinkled at the tinge of burning cinders as we reached the epicenter of the tunnels, and the home to the Surtr. We rounded the last tunnel and the walls opened up to the expanse of the underground city that teemed with life. Lava drifted in lazy pools around the perimeter, dipping back into the rock and leaving the life-giving energy of its heat to spin the massive turn wheels that powered the way of Surtr life.

"Wow," Will breathed as he stepped out on the long ledge that built a single bridge that was used to enter and leave the city.

Instinctually, I spread my wings, wanting to ride the massive updrafts of heat as I'd done as a child.

Billy straightened and grinned, showing his serrated row of teeth again and beaming with the pride of his people. The Surtr were one of the Jotun and could adapt to any element. I'd never truly understood what that meant until I'd learned that Muspelheim hadn't always been a volcanic planet. What would have melted the flesh from my mortal bones was now a life-giving resource to the adaptive nature of the natives.

Billy spread his arms. "Welcome to Jotunheim."

"Great," Will murmured as we navigated the terrifying walkway that led to the core of the city, "more Norse nonsense for me to remember. Surtr: Minotaurs with shark teeth, check. Muspelheim, planet that doesn't know when to stop producing lava, check. Jotunheim: a mysterious city inside said planet with even more lava."

I snorted and covered my mouth with my hand. It seemed that even though I didn't have my mortal body anymore, I still had some embarrassing traits. Will smirked at me and I nudged him to keep walking. "I'm glad you're keeping track because there's going to be a quiz later."

Billy peered at us from over his shoulder. His spine made him hunch, his body built for long leaps across lava pools. "What's a quiz?"

I gasped. "Oh, a terrifying earth atrocity. They come when you least expect them and leave you rattled for days."

Will nodded, an expression of complete seriousness making his jaw rigid. "Absolutely. You don't want to come across a quiz."

Billy's eyes went wide. "Wow. Good thing I don't have to go to Earth. Life there sounds tough."

We giggled behind our hands while Billy led us into the heart of the city. A part of me was grateful to have my natural form so that I could walk beside Will and make progress towards ending Baldr's hold on my homeworld. As much as I wanted to pretend my brother wasn't my problem, Ragnarök had other plans. I frowned when I noticed the specks of glittering black running through the layers of Jotunheim like gems. "How much longer do we have until we have to evacuate?"

Billy followed my gaze and sighed. "Ragnarök burrows deep and Baldr's forces keep coming. They drill through the caves and try to bypass our traps. Something has their attention and the majority have left, but I have no doubt they'll be back."

My stomach dropped, remembering Tyler and that flash of light in the sky. Will's hand slipped into mine and squeezed.

We continued to wind through the city, the Surtr natives only dropping us curious glances before going about their business. The Surtr were the ones who built Valkyrie spears and armor. Where they were talented at weaponry, they were even more skilled at software. We entered into a room alive with lights and buttons that lined the walls. One Surtr strapped into a revolving chair spun around the room, pressing sequences all at once as if he were Freya smashing buttons until something happened. I didn't realize it was a female until she lifted her goggles and her gleaming ruby eyes caught mine. "Ah, Valerie Frigg. Billy informed us you were wandering the tunnels." She glanced at Will. "And who is this handsome Valiant?"

Will straightened. "Just someone who wants to stop Ragnarök as much as you do."

The female nodded. "Indeed. I'll take all the help we can get." She continued her work and spun through the room, making me dodge out of the way when she rounded towards a panel next to my head.

Billy pulled a lever and made the chair stop. "Now that Val is here, don't you think we should show her?"

The female frowned. "Oh, right. Yes. I suppose." She unbuckled herself and dropped to the ground, her hooves clomping hard against the stone. "This way."

As she pressed another sequence of buttons and a door opened on the other end of the chamber, she gave me a smile. "I see that you don't remember me, child. That's all right. I heard about your run-in with Grimhildr."

I swallowed hard. The sassy Surtr did seem to ring a bell, but my memories refused to surface. Just like when I'd met Will, I simply had gut feelings to base my decisions off of. The feelings swarming in my chest told me I could trust her. "Sorry," I murmured.

She waved my apology away. "Don't be. My name's Ymir. Your mother and I don't always see eye-to-eye on things, but we both love this planet. We loved it enough to keep the most important thing in the universe safe, should it ever fall into the wrong hands."

That made me raise a brow and I glanced at Will. He shrugged. "What could be more important than the Einherjar? Or the Valkyries?"

Ymir grinned. "How about the key to the Bifrost?"

*Y*mir took us through, yet again, more tunnels. My wings twitched as the sensation of being closed in by rock and stone started to get to me.

"Here we are," Ymir said as she stopped at a panel and plugged in a code so fast that I couldn't have even hoped to remember it. She glanced at me and grinned. "Just because I have hooves you think my fingers aren't nimble?"

I fumbled at the constricting wall of my leathers that hugged my ribcage. I missed my old jeans and T-shirts. "You're having way too much fun poking fun at the Valkyrie with amnesia."

Will crossed his arms. "What's behind door number one?"

Ymir pressed the final button and two doors pressed together hissed as they unlatched. When they slowly drifted apart, I drew in a gasp.

A thick glass wall separated us from raw, molten lava. Heat should have been billowing into the room and cooking us alive, but I realized the encasement wasn't glass at all. I walked up to it and ran my fingers over the pristine material.

"Fascinating, isn't it?" Ymir remarked, clearly proud as she straightened. She pressed a hand to the wall and closed her eyes. "I can almost feel the power it took to build this. Such a massive undertaking."

"What's it made of?" Will asked, sounding curious in spite of himself.

"It's a form of diamond, carbon compressed until it's so tightly bound that even heat can't penetrate it." She shrugged. "Perhaps there's a bit of Yggdrasil sap in it as well. A little magic goes a long way."

I pulled my hand away. "Great. So this is a giant grave." I knew what it took to draw Yggdrasil's sap from a soul. The Huldra's honeycomb form had taken merciless sacrifice one after another to build enough power to fuel the Bifrost. The Surtr likely worked in the same fashion, being just another race of the collective Jotun.

"Don't get your feathers all in a bunch," Ymir said and clacked her hoof against the stone. "Valkyries return to this planet after their death, remember? That's plenty of sap for us to work with. Your mother had no use for it, since she can only work with mortal souls, and she wants the Bifrost just as badly as we do."

I raised an eyebrow. "You're telling me that you can get the Bifrost under our control?" That'd be a game changer. Even Ragnarök didn't have control over time and space to that degree. And once Ragnarök was taken care of, perhaps even Asgard could be reclaimed.

I shook my head, finding myself going down the path

of a Valkyrie who served Freya. It wasn't my responsibility to take control back from my brother. I was going to do what needed to be done to give Will the life he deserved, then I was done.

Ymir waved her hand and the wall emanated with a soft blue light, sending the lava parting to reveal the golden hull of a ship. "We have the Gulltop."

A memory triggered at that name. "It's what fuels the Bifrost." Or, at least, it's what used to power it before Dalia used whatever souls she could find. Realization swept through me. The Heimdall line, that was why they controlled the Bifrost. Only they had enough darkness and the capability to devour souls and fuel something as powerful as the Bifrost without the help of the Gulltop.

Will paced in front of the massive wall. "How do we get to it?" The lava swarmed around the Gulltop, revealing hints of tunnels that acted as release valves for the pressure, keeping the flow of lava constant.

Ymir laughed. "You can't drain this chamber, not without blasting through the vent chambers and being disintegrated by the lava that would be released. This is lava from the heart of Muspelheim. Not even a Surtr or a Valkyrie could survive it. The Bifrost is a terrifying force and the Heimdall who controls it can only do small jumps. She can't send entire armies between worlds. If she had the Gulltop, she could do just that."

I frowned. "What if *we* had the Bifrost?" The original Bifrost worked not only in space, but in time as well. I could take Will back to before any of this happened. Perhaps I could even prevent his mother from selling his soul to the Norn.

That would mean that I'd never have met Will in the first place and dread sank to my bones, but I knew if I ever did get control of the Bifrost, that's exactly what I'd have to do. Ragnarök would never have been triggered, Will would get his human life he deserved... but what would happen to me?

Ymir frowned at me as I struggled to keep my face under control. I wasn't very good at hiding my emotions. I cleared my throat and pushed hair that escaped the tight band of my headdress aside. The armor seemed to summon itself the longer I was in my Valkyrie form. I looked down, seeing leathery boots wrapped over my thighs. My spear hinted its presence with a flurry of embers at my fingertips.

"What did you have in mind?" Ymir asked, still watching me with that scrutinizing gaze that I had a feeling didn't miss a thing. "There's a reason we encased the Gulltop behind impenetrable diamond and surrounded it with molten lava."

I bit my lip and looked to Will for strength. He was the one soul who was innocent in all of this. He didn't deserve to be here with stress and fear glimmering in the rainbow sheen of his armor that crusted over his body. I wasn't the only one on edge. "Where is the Bifrost now?" I asked instead.

Ymir pulled a device from her tool belt that was about the only garment on her Surtr body. The rest of her was covered in a light sheen of fur that kept her otherwise decent to my human-accustomed eyes. Her brows furrowed as she watched the screen. "It's still over the city, but its cold signature is growing. It's trying to jump something." Her ruby gaze met mine. "Something big."

GODS

$\mathscr{Y}$mir took us to the mortal transitional quarters, a place similar to the rooms on the Einherjar designed for Immortals shedding their Immortal skin. I brightened when I spotted Mr. Jefferson.

My history teacher couldn't have looked more at home in the small nursery where children Surtr and human alike played together. He laughed when they collectively grabbed his book and tried to rip it from his hands.

"Another story, Jeff-Jeff!" said a small boy with two little horns that curled over his forehead.

A human girl tugged on one of the horns and got him to release the prize. "No! He said he was going to show me how to dance!"

Mr. Jefferson still had his human form, and I wondered if he'd ever let it go. He seemed content in his skin, even if the tell-tale sign of fire streaked through his veins. He didn't try to hide it here, and the Surtr children with human faces did the same. The fire-blood of Muspelheim transformed them and molded them, making them the only creatures I knew who could hold a fire in themselves better than a Valkyrie.

Mr. Jefferson's smile grew when he spotted us. "Ah! Val, and Will? What a surprise."

Will blinked, and I realized that he didn't know Mr. Jefferson had been an Immortal. I laughed and prodded him in the ribs. "C'mon, don't look so surprised."

Will shook his head. "Is everyone I know inhuman?"

Mr. Jefferson stood and shook off the children that clung to his legs. He coaxed them with promises of more stories if they would be good and go with Ymir to complete the rest of their daily lessons.

I expected the clinically scientific Surtr to be offended by the children, but Ymir drew the girl up onto her hip and laughed when the child tugged on her more impressive horns. "Come, children. Let's leave Jeff-Jeff to talk with our guests."

"Will you do the melting trick again?" a boy asked hopefully as he trotted at her heels.

She smiled and a wicked gleam glimmered in her eye. "Only if you behave. Now come along."

I watched in fascination as the children swarmed around her, screeching with delight when she ran a finger along the wall and left a molten streak in her wake. So that was the melting trick.

"She does like to show off," Mr. Jefferson said with a touch of fondness to his voice. He situated himself at a short table designed for much smaller Surtr and folded his hands. "Now, what brings you two here? Was it just Ragnarök?" His gaze fell to my pouch. "Or did you have something about Yggdrasil to share?"

I slipped into one of the chairs that was barely knee-high. My wings draped over the back and grazed the floor. Instinct born of the endless chiding from my mentors had taught me to pick the appendages back up, but I couldn't even lift a finger right now. I was so tired and weighed down by secrets. I didn't want to hide them from Mr. Jefferson.

"I went to Yggdrasil," I said, my voice low with the admission. "I'm a Frigg and I have the same powers as a Heimdall." Something deep within me told me that I'd taken my one and only shot at setting foot on Yggdrasil's soil. After my thievery, I was not welcome back there again.

I glanced at Will, guilt returning with the knowledge that if I failed, he'd never get to find peace there. Even if I was doomed to wander the world for eternity, he wasn't born into this fate. He'd been betrayed by the one supposed to care for him the most.

Will joined us at the round table littered with rocks that I now realized glowed red. The table itself was a shade of limestone, strong enough not to be blistered by the fiery toys. I picked one up, indulging in the surge of blistering heat that ran up my arm. As a Valkyrie, I communed with fire. It's why the Surtr and the Valkyrie were a good match.

"Do you believe Ragnarök can be stopped?" Will asked.

Mr. Jefferson stroked his chin, managing to look like an ordinary teacher as if we were sitting in his classroom at Mattsfield High. That life seemed so far away and so long ago. "No. I don't." When our faces fell, he lifted a pointed finger. "However, I do believe it can be buried. The universe is a large place and there are pockets deep enough for even a mass of that size to be put to rest."

I continued to turn the ember over in my fingers, keeping myself busy so I didn't go for the more precious treasure in my pouch. The fruit of Yggdrasil lingered a soft melody that drifted in the background of my senses, and I knew the longer I kept it in this world, the more it would wish to return home. "Isn't that precisely what Freya and Odin have done during past cycles?"

Mr. Jefferson stiffened. "That's what I suspected. They don't admit to past cycles. Until now, that had been my theory."

I bit my lip. I hadn't intended to spill any of my mother's secrets, but I let the guilt wash away. Leaving the rest of the universe in the dark and trying to manage Ragnarök all on her own was precisely why she'd failed. I wasn't going to make the same mistake. "She told me that Ragnarök is the culmination of suffering and darkness that gave Immortals life in the first place." I left out the part where she and Odin were actually its initial creators, having been the birth of Immortality in the first place. I would leave Mr. Jefferson to figure out that one on his own. "After it was done devouring the world, she trapped it in a pocket of space and time."

Mr. Jefferson nodded gravely. "That would line up with my theory. The power of a Frigg and a goddess like Freya would be enough to trap the beast in such a prison."

I leaned over the table and my wings draped over my shoulders. "Do you think we could replicate it before it devours the world?"

Mr. Jefferson hummed. "It has already begun its feed on Muspelheim and it'll stay here until it's drained the life-force of fallen Valkyries."

My stomach lurched. "What'll happen to them?"

He shrugged. "It seems Baldr made use of them as foot soldiers, but now that the majority of Freya's forces have fled, I suspect he's begun Ragnarök's feed."

Will scratched his nails against the table and growled his frustration. "What does this Baldr have to do with Ragnarök? I swear, this bastard plagues me in every area of my life. First he twists my mother with promises of Immortality until she becomes a monster. Now he wants to play god of Ragnarök? What does he gain by destroying the world?"

Mr. Jefferson's eyes gleamed with the power of his race. I wasn't fooled by his collected demeanor. Ragnarök had shaken his race to the core. "Let me ask you a question, Will. When you look at Valerie, what do you see?"

Will leaned back and glanced at me. "What do you mean?"

"Just tell me how she makes you feel. Then try to tell me why she makes you feel that way."

Will shifted uncomfortably, and even through the gold hue of his Valiant magic, I could have sworn I saw his cheeks tint red in a blush. "Valerie is the only light in my life. She's been there for me when no one else was. When I feel hopeless or like everything around me is about to collapse, I can just look into her eyes and live in the present. It's what's kept me sane."

Rocked by how much I meant to him, I wanted to tell him he was wrong. I wasn't the light in his life. I was the darkness that had blotted it out.

"And why do you think that is?" Mr. Jefferson asked thoughtfully. "What is it about her?"

Will looked into my eyes and smiled. "It's the love we share. Even through death, it's kept our bond strong. Even through the loss of memory and the loss of our bodies, my love for her will never fail."

I swallowed hard. "Will."

He took my hand. "There's nothing wrong with me loving you," he insisted. "If it's about Tyler, it's fine. I was childish to be jealous over it. He's been there for you a hell of a lot longer than I ever have been. How could he not fall in love with you?"

Tears sizzled in my eyes and I was grateful I didn't have to wipe them away. A Valkyrie never cried, for tears never survived the heat of our nature. "But you deserve so much better," I insisted. "It's my fault you're a Valiant. I failed you. You should hate me."

"What?" He slipped off his chair and knelt at my side. "Why do you insist to place this burden on yourself?"

"She's right," Mr. Jefferson said, the validation making my teeth grind together. I wasn't sure if I was ready for this, but I couldn't fight Ragnarök if Will followed me blindly into the fire. I needed him to let me go for the next step of my plan to work. "Freya and the Norn have a deal. The Norn entice humans with Immortality and the Valkyrie reap the souls. Of course there were disagreements over how many souls the Valkyrie would get until it turned into an all-out war. Baldr now leads the Norn and Freya fights for every soul she can get." His ruby gaze landed on me, burning with merciless fury. "Ragnarök was due to come, be it from Valerie's love or some other event. Fate cannot be avoided. Freya knew that when the echoes of Ragnarök began to spread across the universe."

Will shook his head. "So what does that have to do with me? Why does this put any blame onto Val?"

Mr. Jefferson turned his gaze to Will. "Don't you see? Valerie is a Frigg. She could have reaped your soul and prevented Ragnarök's return. She's strong enough to imprison it, but she let you go. She allowed you to kill her sister and become a Valiant." He sneered. "Now you're useless and just as damned as the rest of us."

Ymir appeared from the doorway, as if summoned by Mr. Jefferson's rudeness, and startled me by slapping him on the back of the head. "Jeffra!" she sniped, using his native name. "What's the matter with you? I thought you were supposed to be good with children."

The fire left his gaze and he rolled his shoulders back. "My apologies. I simply was taken off guard by learning a dark truth I'd always suspected about Freya." He gave Ymir a raised brow. "Did you abandon the children just to come and berate me?"

She glowered. "They're with Billy. He's just as good a mentor as you or I."

That surprised me. I'd always viewed Billy as a comrade, but it seems after a hundred years, he'd grown into a position of respect and leadership, guiding young Surtr just as he'd done for me.

Satisfied, Mr. Jefferson nodded. "Very well. I shall retire to my quarters, if you'll excuse me."

We watched him leave and Ymir gave us an apologetic smile. "I don't know what's gotten into him." She sighed, then gave us a wistful smile. "I'll show you two to your rooms."

We followed Ymir down the corridors and I'd stopped trying to keep track of where we were. If Ragnarök chased me right now, it would win, because there was no way I could find my way out again.

"Why do you think Mr. Jefferson asked me to clarify why I loved you?"

I shrugged and made an effort to keep my wings from trailing the ground behind me. "Perhaps he was pointing out that you're in love with your own death."

He shook his head. "No. There's more to it than that." Will took my hand as we walked. I liked being close to him, but right now I just wanted to pull away. Even after everything we'd learned, he still hadn't come to the conclusion that I was toxic to him.

"You're light. You're warmth. He was trying to show me that you're everything good." He gave me a raised brow. "Perhaps you're everything Freya was supposed to be."

"Yeah, so?" Freya had told me that I was all her love, which meant I was the culmination of her failure and weakness.

"Then what does that make Baldr?"

I stopped in my tracks. Ymir and Will paused and stared at me. "If I'm light, then Baldr is dark." I met Will's gaze. "But I'm darkness too, Will. The only difference between my brother and I is that I'm trying to stop Ragnarök."

Will grinned. "Maybe not. Maybe you're just going about it differently."

Ymir piped up. "Are you telling me that Baldr thinks he's trying to save the universe?" She buckled over and laughed. "That's a good one."

I chewed on my lip before making a decision. "I think Will's right." When Ymir stared at me like I was nuts, I flared my wings, hoping it gave me a sense of authority. "Do you have any hologram screens I can use?"

*J*t felt very twenty-first century to call up my brother, but that's exactly what I'd decided to do. If I'd gotten him wrong all this time and his goals were the same as mine, at least on the larger spectrum, perhaps there was some reasoning with him.

Standing in the hologram room with a three-sixty wall that wrapped around me, I glanced at Will through the translucent screen. He nodded, offering me encouragement and strength, but staying off the platform so Baldr couldn't see him. No matter my hopes, Baldr would only use him against me again.

The extravagant dining hall appeared when Baldr picked up the call. I swallowed, recognizing the luxurious low drapes and unending platter of delicacies.

An Immortal didn't need to eat, and the display of fresh fruit and wine only boasted Baldr's stature. Asgard was alive and well and as of yet, untouched by Ragnarök.

"Sister," he said, his voice already grating on my last nerve. "How unexpected. Have you called to plea for surrender?"

I glowered and flared my wings, which only served to make him laugh. Before he could comment on my Immortal form, I summoned my spear in a burst of flame. My powers came to me so much easier with my feet on Muspelheim soil. Lava and the magic that burned through my veins roared to life and whispered the desire to burn. Flame always changed anything it touched down to the very molecular level. If I found myself face-to-face with Baldr again, I'd show him exactly what kind of power I had for those who crossed me. "You attack our mother, you attack me, but you yourself remain lazing about on Asgard. Why is that?"

He examined his nails. "Oh, I don't know. Perhaps I'm bored with the thought of such an easy victory." He lowered his hand and grinned. "Of course, it's exactly what I expected. I'm good at understanding my opponent's weakness."

I gripped my spear, resisting the urge to form a portal and jump right through the screen and impale his face. "You wanted me here for this, why?"

He laughed. "Ah, yes. That was a fun trick. Your love is your weakness, dear sister." His laughter faded. "As it is mine."

That got my attention. "You're capable of love?"

He clutched at his chest. "Oh, how you wound me." He waved over someone who was off the screen. The same graceful Valkyrie I'd seen before that seemed to like to fawn all over him now draped herself over his chest. "What is it, Baldr?" Her voice came through the speakers just as musical and pure as the rare selection of Valkyries who inherited our mother's grace and beauty at its finest.

He ran a finger across her neck before gripping it and putting her in a chokehold. "Would you care to show my sister what happens to those I love?"

Her eyes went wide, but she didn't struggle. She gurgled something, but Baldr didn't let go. Then her eyes flared with flame, a warning sign that a Valkyrie was about to draw on the strength of the powers of Muspelheim that ran through her blood. For the same reason we didn't need food or water, we didn't even need to breathe if we accepted the raw magic that gave us our bodies.

Baldr growled. "I gave you an order."

"Stop this!" I shrieked. I didn't even know if it was possible for a Valkyrie to deny herself the life-giving force that came naturally to us from birth. "What point are you trying to prove?"

He responded by wrapping his other hand around the Valkyrie's throat. She twisted at an odd angle until he squeezed hard enough for her neck to snap. The light immediately died in her eyes, fading as fast as the light of her body.

I watched in horror as Baldr drew shadows from her flesh. He inhaled what was left of her soul that should have returned to the pits of Muspelheim.

I rocked back on my heels. Baldr had just shown me what we were capable of. We were Freya's children, but we also belonged to Odin. That made us gods of another kind. Instead of giving life... we could take it for ourselves.

Images of Tyler flashed, those tell-tale shadows creeping across his skin. Each black rune that marred his perfect body was a soul he'd devoured.

I stared down at the rune that stretched an ugly scar across my hand and realization swept through me.

"Yes. You get it now." Baldr dropped the Valkyrie's body to the ground and it fell with a soft *thud*. "You understand what we are."

Baldr didn't care if Ragnarök devoured the world... because those with this ugly power would be all that remained once it was done.

My mouth went dry and I licked my lips. "What are we?" I asked, my voice raw.

"Our parents have staved off Ragnarök so many times that they finally started to become like it. They've been devouring souls longer than we've even been alive. It makes sense that we'd inherit their darkest secret and turn it against them."

I didn't want to listen to Baldr's logic. "So you *want* Ragnarök to destroy the universe? Are you insane?"

He shook his head. "You think so small, my sister. We let Ragnarök do its work, but we won't let it finish." He twirled the wisp of shadow around his finger, commanding it to dance for him across his knuckles. "Haven't you tried feeding from Ragnarök itself?"

My eyes went wide. "Feeding?"

He laughed. "I know you've fed before. I see the rune."

He hid my hand behind me. There had to be some mistake. "I haven't fed on anyone."

He gave me a raised brow. "No? Not even that human you supposedly loved so much? Where is he now? Have you asked him if he feels like something is missing?"

I glanced at Will and he was shaking his head. I knew what he was thinking. *Don't let him tell you this is your fault. I'm fine. I'm here.*

But Will wasn't fine. He wasn't all here. Every time I looked at him, I saw how fractured he was. I'd thought what was missing was his mortality. I'd been wrong. It was a piece of his soul.

I licked my lips again, desperately wishing I had something to drink. That's when I ran my fingers across the hidden fruit still in my pouch and hope blossomed in my chest. Whatever I'd taken from Will, this could give it back to him.

"Sister. You are indeed hopeless. It was probably an accident. That's why he's still alive. You could have taken everything, but you only took what you needed."

What I needed. The truth in that statement shook me to the core. Ever since Will's death I'd begun to regain my memories. I'd found the strength to overcome Grimhildr's programming and I'd even been able to step through space and time with ease. Such a leap in ability wasn't because of some inherent strength. I'd fed on Will's soul.

I squeezed my eyes shut. "I called you because I wanted to work together. I want to stop Ragnarök and find a truce." I opened my eyes and met his. The man who looked back at me was wild and uncontrollable. He stood tall and proud, pensively watching me as if he were Odin himself, but I sensed the frustration and pent-up aggression in the lines of his jaw. "What is it that you really want, Baldr?"

"I told you before," he chided. "I want Sam."

I shook my head. "And you know that she's gone."

He huffed a laugh. "Haven't you been paying attention?" He turned to the body that had already started to harden. He swept his fingers over it, releasing the shadows that he'd drawn in.

125

My entire body went still as I watched. The glittering black was reminiscent of Ragnarök as it twisted and moved like tiny claws as it gripped the Valkyrie and lifted her up. It burrowed into her and made her convulse.

Then her eyes opened.

At first her irises were the purest of black, and then the shadows faded, leaving the ember purity of a Valkyrie renewed. "Baldr," she breathed, her face softening into relief. "You brought me back."

I balked. Once again I searched for Will through the screen, but he was gone. My blood ran cold. Was he afraid of me now? I couldn't deny that I was exactly like my brother. The only difference was that one of us had embraced what we were.

Gods.

"*Y*ou know how to reach me when you're ready to accept our fate."

Baldr's last words still shook me to the core. I'd been staring at the blank hologram screen for what seemed like an eternity before Ymir gently took my hand. "Aerie?"

Calling me by Tyler's nickname for me jolted me back into awareness. He was still up in the Einherjar fighting for me while I was supposed to be figuring this all out. The truth, however, wasn't so easy to unravel. According to Baldr, stopping Ragnarök was a simple matter of accepting what I was. If I fed on it, if I drew its darkness into myself, I could save everyone... but I feared what would happen to me.

"I can't do it," I whispered.

My hands shook and Ymir drew me off the platform. "No one is asking you to."

"What's going on here?" Mr. Jefferson snapped. His veins illuminated in the dim light with harsh ruby tones. "Will told me to tell Valerie not to feed on Ragnarök. Did I hear him right?"

I blinked at him. "Where's Will?"

Mr. Jefferson frowned. "How should I know? He rushed past me and shouted orders at me as if I hadn't been his teacher for the past two years. No respect these days."

I looked to Ymir whose features had gone unreadable. Even if I had no memories of her, that seemed suspicious. Ymir was the kind of Surtr who always had an opinion and always knew what was going on. "What aren't you saying? Where's Will gone?"

She released me. "I suspect he's gone to the Gulltop."

"What?" I asked. "Why?"

She released a long breath. "If he thinks the Bifrost will save you from having to sacrifice yourself to save the rest of us, then he's going to break the seal on the Gulltop for you to do just that."

I ran as fast as I could, but I didn't get very far. I cursed when I reached the first split in the tunnels. "Which way?" I demanded.

I'd dragged Ymir with me. Even though she protested, I wasn't going to let her go. "I can't tell you that," she bit out.

I gripped her wrist until her bones grated together. She winced, but clacked her hoof. "Yes you can," I insisted. "Will is hanging on by a thread. If I'm going to restore his mortality, then I need him alive. There's no telling what breaking the Gulltop seal will do to what's left of his soul."

She ground her teeth but didn't seem inclined to budge. "He loves you. Allow him to protect you the only way he knows how."

The tunnels shook and a male cry echoed through the corridors. I released Ymir as desperation made black stars sprinkle across my vision. "What was that?"

The lights wavered, turning red, then blue and going into a low hum as energy swept through Jotunheim.

I was too late.

Will was dead.

I was already in my Valkyrie form. I'd lost my mortal flesh. I'd lost Sam.

Now I'd lost Will.

I let go of the last hold I'd kept on my Immortality. Fire unlocked in my soul and ignited, releasing my internal rage and darkness I'd kept at bay for so long.

Tyler wasn't here to save me this time. He understood my darkness better than anyone, and now I knew why. The dark scar running along my arm blistered and solidified, becoming a permanent scar as the remnants of Will's soul found me and absorbed into my body. Feeling the surge of power that gave me only enraged me more. I was Will's death and no matter how much everyone tried to tell me none of this was my fault... I was the one to blame.

Tears sizzled into steam in my eyes and my wings caught fire. Ymir screamed in the distance, but I couldn't decipher her words. Even a Surtr couldn't withstand the full force of my rage and grief. I was the child of two gods, and not everything that was good about them. I was the birth of their secrets and their sin. I was an abomination.

I should have joined Ragnarök in that moment and merged with its glittering black fingers that devoured this world, but one small piece of sanity found its way into my mind.

Why did Will just sacrifice himself?

I ran through the corridors and followed the scent of his sacrifice, coming upon the chamber to the Gulltop completely emptied. There was nothing left of him, but the evidence of what he'd done was in the massive split in the wall that diverted the lava through the venting corridors that were intended to reroute the lava, but he'd opened them all. He'd gone inside those tunnels and put a crack in each one, being devoured by flame to release the final seal on the Gulltop.

My fingernails bit into my palms and every muscle in me shook with the wrecking grief that he'd do this to me. He couldn't be reborn, not if I had devoured his soul. I was his curse, and now he was a part of me. That wasn't enough.

But the Gulltop, it rested on the bottom of the chamber lopsided with a single panel glowing with warning. I approached it and stared at the buttons.

Ymir drifted behind me, followed by Billy and Mr. Jefferson, as well as a small herd of Surtr I didn't recognize. Some of them had weapons, and I didn't underestimate the primal spears they pointed my way. This race was the one that had fashioned Freya's spear and given the weapon such powerful cruelty. I had no doubt their own weapons had a few secrets in their software.

"Help me open it," I growled. My voice grated through my throat with the pain I couldn't express. Shadows licked over the flames sprouting across my arms. My Valkyrie armor was having a hard time holding up against the onslaught and hardened into black leathers.

Ymir stepped forward. "The Gulltop was caged for good reason," she insisted. "One wrong move and you could change everything."

My vision flared as flames licked in the backs of my eyes. "That's precisely what I want to do." When she gave me a blank stare, I motioned to the cracked and burned surroundings. "Is this the timeline you want? Ragnarök on our doorstep, Freya and Odin trapped on the Einherjar with the Valkyries who have survived? Your people hiding in caves awaiting Ragnarök and the Skuld to finally find you?"

Her lower lip began to tremble. "No, of course not, but—"

"Then open this door," I snapped.

She glanced over her shoulder at Mr. Jefferson who hesitated, then gave her a slow deliberate nod. Billy motioned to protest, but Mr. Jefferson lowered his hand. "She's right." His words were so low that they were barely audible. "This is not the timeline we should be living." His eyes met mine, matching my rage with their fiery red. "Daughter of Freya, daughter of Odin, you inherit the Gulltop, the Bifrost, even Asgard with every right. Baldr is not our ruler." He knelt to one knee. "You are our Queen and I recognize you with the authority of all the Surtr have to offer."

Ymir stiffened, but finally relented and knelt as well. The rest of the Surtr followed suit, dropping to a knee one-by-one.

My wings flared. "Thank you," I said, then pressed my hand against the blazing metal of the Gulltop. "Now help me fix this."

THE GULLTOP

I didn't think about the consequences of going back in time. If I stopped to consider what I was doing, I wouldn't have the strength.

I climbed into the confined space of the Gulltop alone. Buttons glowed to life and there was just enough space for one more person.

I gave Ymir a hard glare through the hatch. "You're coming with me."

She went pale, but climbed in.

Only a Surtr would know how to operate this thing. Like most of the technology that dictated the Immortal world, I suspected it was Ymir who had built it.

Confirming my suspicions, she plucked away at the buttons and the hatch closed in behind us. "When I made the Bifrost, I thought that I was helping our race. Traveling through the universe and colonizing other planets was our dream."

I listened patiently. This was the kind of information I needed in order to save the world. "The Bifrost was a prototype?"

She nodded. "It's still my best work yet. Only one device can link into the slipstream of space and time." She patted the hull of the Gulltop fondly. "But this device can enforce it, grows upon it and manipulates it. Instead of just transporting the individuals in the room through space, the Gulltop opens time as well."

I nodded. "I know exactly where... when, I want to go."

Ymir gave me a mournful look. Her hand rested on mine, her red-hot claws feeling cold against the raw heat that burned inside of me. "I warn you, time cannot often be changed. And when it can, the consequences aren't typically what you'd expect." She placed my hand on a sequence of buttons. "But you and I are not the same. Perhaps you will succeed where I failed."

I wondered what attempts Ymir had made that had

resulted in the permanent seal of the Gulltop behind deadly lava. "What makes you say you failed?"

She gave me a weak smile. "The Jotun are the result of my experiments. Instead of Terraforming planets to suit our needs, I experimented on freshly Immortal bodies, mine included. We were supposed to adapt to any planet we called home. Instead, we became enslaved to it and changed on a fundamental level that we cannot survive without it." Her gaze went distant as she ran her fingers over the length of her horns. "The Surtr didn't always look like this. We were once beautiful, but when I bound myself and my clan to Muspelheim, I learned that we could never leave." Her eyes glimmered. "Until Freya came into the picture, that is. She gave us Yggdrasil's sap and Muspelheim itself fueled Jotunheim with new power. Some of us are able to resume our more natural human forms. Without Freya, though, we all would have been trapped here forever, doomed to Muspelheim's fate." She drew out a vial of glittering gold liquid and popped it open. She downed it in two seconds flat and her form twisted and shimmered. Her horns retreated into her head and her skin lost its metallic, red hue. When she fully transformed into a beautiful woman, I openly stared. She laughed. "Oh, right." She popped open the hatch at the floor which revealed an assortment of packages. She opened one and shimmied into the tight suit. She offered me a bag. "Helps with the distortions. Think of it as anti-g-force. Acceleration is always a component of time, and when you're going in reverse, it has a Hel of a punch."

I grimaced at it, then flexed my wings. They couldn't extend all the way before hitting sensitive machinery. "I'll pass."

She shrugged and returned the bag to the hatch before flipping the lid closed. "Suit yourself."

She cracked her knuckles, then started dancing her fingers across the glowing lights. All she was missing was her revolving chair.

I watched, mesmerized, and then a hologram screen popped in front of our faces, revealing the watchful Surtr standing outside the hull.

She cleared her throat, then hit an orange button. "Our Queen would like to say something before we embark." When I widened my eyes at her, she motioned for me to speak.

I sighed. I hated speeches. "I'm sorry for everything that's happened. My mother is supposed to protect this planet and its people. You are our allies, and you don't deserve for Ragnarök to be breathing down your necks. I'm going back to the beginning when this all started and make sure the timeline is corrected. Wish me luck."

A cheer sounded before the screen blipped off. "Well done." She gave me a wink. "You'll make a fine Queen." She pointed at scroll knob with eight runes glimmering beside it. I recognize the Norse style merged with the modern date system. "Plug in when you want to go. Just remember, once you successfully change the timeline, it'll take the space-time net a period to adjust. You won't be able to use it again—not in this lifetime, anyway."

So, no pressure then. Great.

J'd been watching Will ever since he'd been assigned to me. His first life was his dedication to the Norn and the first moment he'd appeared on our scanners. I'd been so young then that I hadn't understood what it meant to be dedicated to the Norn, but I knew the date by heart. Those Norse runes were etched into my memory as the day I'd gone from being a child to becoming a fledgling Valkyrie.

I dialed in the date: February 4th, 1955.

The Gulltop hummed to life, singing that familiar high-pitched scream that was all too familiar. When the Einherjar had sent me to Earth and fitted me with a human body, the same invading sensations rattled my bones, but this wasn't just travel through space. My Frigg powers reacted as the Gulltop drew its strength from me. The Bifrost was powered by the souls trapped on Asgard, but the Gulltop had no such resource. It was now powered through me.

I sensed Dalia when the Gulltop made its connection to the sister ship. Her shouts rang in the background of my senses, warning Baldr that the Bifrost was being manipulated. I grinned, because there was nothing that he could do about this. He wasn't a Frigg and he had spurned the Surtr, the one race that could have helped him gain control over time itself.

I was glad the Surtr were on my side. I wanted to tell Ymir as much, how much I appreciated her help, but the Gulltop's screech ended and my vision went black as pain streaked through my body.

Another scream sounded, and this time I realized it was my own. Every atom in my body protested the reverse movement through time as the Gulltop gained momentum, ripping into me and pulling out the dark powers of my Frigg nature to unseat us from the present.

How ironic, I thought, that this was how I would save Will. He'd always loved the present.

---

*S*candinavia, 1920

The hilltop where Will had been dedicated as a child was just as I remembered it, but my memories were from a grainy hologram screen that had spied on the aftermath of the contract Leanne had made with the Norn. The darkness that had cemented the bond had distorted the image, leaving me wondering what Will had looked like as a child in this life. I'd been submerged in my training at that time, Tyler close on my heels trying to make sure I learned how to defend myself against the power of the Norn. He had firsthand experience with them and it was his fear of them that had driven me. I'd been so focused on protecting myself and learning the skills I would need that I hadn't even paid attention to Will during his first, short life.

Now, though, I marveled at the serene calm of the

wavy hills topped with bright grass that made it look more like a velvet carpet than something born of nature. The sky glowed with a healthy blue and puffy clouds lazily danced across the horizon.

I'd arrived during the cheery part of the day. Wildlife bounced through crags and a chill wind tangled invisible fingers through my hair.

Then a twig crunched behind me and I whirled to find Ymir grinning. Panic filled me as I searched for the Gulltop. Where was it?

"Relax," she said. "This is how it works."

"How do we get back to our time?" I asked as dizziness swept over me. My feathers brushed my shoulders and I startled, nearly forgetting that even though I was surrounded by Earth's air and soil-scent, I was still a creature of Muspelheim.

"The Gulltop hasn't moved, it's still in the heart of Jotunheim. It's transported our bodies through time and space and we'll be yanked back like a rubber band when you call for it."

"And how do I call for it?" I asked.

She paled. "You mean you don't know? It's the same way that you got us here."

I grimaced. "You put far too much faith in me, Ymir."

She sighed and stepped through the grass, but then she stopped and curled her toes. "This feels amazing." When I glowered at her, she laughed. "Don't worry. I'm sure you'll figure it out." She pointed at an assortment of vertical stones atop the highest hill. Tufts of moss and grass stuck out of its sides. "I assume that's where we're going? I sense something familiar there."

I sensed it too. The pull of a portal drew me to the place that housed the weight of suffering and pain—an Immortal's cocktail for power.

"Come. Let's check it out before Leanne arrives." I marched up the hill and Ymir followed me.

She was a scientist, which meant that her calculating eyes were documenting every step of this journey. She should have been terrified, even just a little bit, but everything seemed to fascinate her. I remembered the first time I'd come to earth, how the abundance of nature and life mesmerized me. Even without my memories, and the addition of a few new ones thanks to Grimhildr, I recognized how special this place was. Humans had no idea how good they had it.

A path of cobblestones and footprints led me to the top of the hill which was more of a rundown temple to the Norse gods. Fresh offerings of mint and flowers settled on the offering stone and I stared at it. Leanne came here often.

Ymir bent and examined the offering. "Do the Norn eat this?"

I laughed. "No. I suspect that humans have their own idea of what the Norn want." The Vikings were the closest to true followers of the Norn. Sacrifice and constant bloodshed were what had given them a place in history, and what had kept Immortals like the Norn going strong for centuries.

"Leanne is going to dedicate Will. I need to stop her." I sat on the stones and stared at the sky. It would only be a few more hours before she'd make her way up the cobbled path. I flexed my wings. There was one thing about being in my native form. She would listen to what I had to say.

Ymir hid in the bushes by the time Leanne arrived. I'd planned out exactly what I was going to say. The crazy woman I remembered didn't care a speck for Will or his future. She was coming here to kill her son, and I was going to do what Grimhildr should have done. Wipe her mind, make her a vegetable, and then I'd make sure Will would find a new home that cared what happened to him.

The shy, wide-eyed woman who crested the hill wasn't how I'd imagined the terrifying creature that would be willing to give her son as sacrifice to the Norn. She stared at me as the blood drained from her face and she clutched a baby to her chest.

"Leanne," I said, hoping to win her over by showing that I knew her name.

She looked more like a frightened rabbit ready to bolt. She froze and her mouth bobbed open and closed, but no words came out.

I shrank my wings to my back as far as I could and crouched as I offered a hand. "It's all right. You don't have to be afraid." I tried to remind myself that this woman was evil beyond evil, but she looked so terri-fied. I managed a smile.

Shaking, she unlocked from her frozen stance and tugged an amulet from underneath her blouse. *"Ofre."* Sacrifice.

My mind worked to translate her tongue, instantly

replacing the Danish with English that I was more accustomed to.

I didn't know if I was capable of speaking her language, but I tried anyway.

I cleared my throat and then flinched when a soft hum swept through my body. I glanced back at the brush where Ymir was hiding, only seeing two eyes peeking at me over the foliage. She held up a device that blinked.

I turned back to the woman whose gaze hadn't left my wings. She was still as white as a sheet. "Leanne," I tried again, this time my lips wrapping around an unfamiliar accent as her language and muscle training of how to form her words downloaded into my brain, "I know why you're here."

She startled. "You speak my language?"

I relaxed, glad that Ymir was able to pull through for me. Trying to talk to Leanne without speaking the same language would have proved difficult. "That's not the question you should be asking."

Her gaze went to my wings again. "You've come for my son's sacrifice?" She pulled the child away from her bosom and offered the boy. I melted when I saw Will's face. Little eyes opened, revealing chestnut irises that had always held me captive.

"No," I snapped, and she clutched the baby back to her chest. I forced my anger to simmer in the low heat of my core that begged to be set free. This woman didn't deserve explanations. Here she was freely offering her child to me. "I've come to ask you not to sacrifice your son."

Her eyes brimmed with tears. "But, he is sickly." She took a brave step forward and I knew it cost her. Her knees wobbled, but she stood her ground. "You're a Valkyrie, yes? Does Freya not demand my son's life, just as she's taken my daughter's?"

My wings flared of their own accord, the feathers scraping against stone and sweeping away the small offerings on the pedestal. Leanne shrank into herself in fear. "A daughter?"

She nodded vigorously. "I would not expect such a warrior as yourself to know of it. Freya does not honor those who die from sickly illness and succumb to weakness." She squeezed her eyes shut as if trying to block out the memories. "I vowed, should I ever have a child again, I would make sure they lived forever and earned a place in Valhalla." She clutched at me with her free hand. "Please. Do not let this child be lost too. He has the same illness."

That's when I sensed the darkness in the child that had been masked by my own rage. I wrapped my fingers around the bundle and Leanne released him.

Holding the baby who cried against my overwhelming warmth, my heart crushed under the inevitability I hadn't expected.

It was just as Leanne had said. I sensed a biological flaw in this child, one that could not be undone. I could knit flesh anew, build new bodies for Immortal souls to inhabit, but I could not mend that which was broken. Tears sizzled in my eyes as I returned the child.

There was something to be said about humans who died of illness. Such suffering weighed down a soul so that even they could not return to Yggdrasil.

If I prevented Leanne from bonding Will's soul to the Norn, he would die in a few short years anyway, denied Yggdrasil and the life I wanted for him.

No matter what I did, I couldn't save him.

JUST A BITE

*P*inned with indecision, Leanne asked me over and over again what she must do. If she could not bind her son to the Norn, how else could she save him?

I had no answer for her. I also couldn't explain that she would turn into a twisted creature unrecognizable from the kind, fretful woman I saw before me now. She was a victim in all of this just as much as the rest of us, just as much as the innocent child in her arms.

Eventually I gave in to the hum of grief in my soul, inwardly activating my connection to the Gulltop and hoping I hadn't done anything to change this timeline. I needed another shot to get this right.

Ymir and I vanished from Scandinavia, from 1955, and returned to the heat of Muspelheim.

*I*f I couldn't save Will by undoing the Norn's curse before it even began, I had to think deeper.

"What if I stop Will from unlocking the seal to the Gulltop in the first place?" I asked Ymir as we huddled in the cramped confines of the time-traveling ship.

She shrugged. "You could try that, but the moment you did the timeline would be rerouted and we would be stuck in a timeline where the Gulltop is still inaccessible."

I growled. "Why did you seal it away in the first place? We need it to stop Baldr, especially if he tries anything." Having time travel on our side gave us a distinct advantage I wasn't ready to give up. It wouldn't matter if I saved Will, only to lose him again to Baldr's insane plan to release Ragnarök on the universe. The bastard actually thought that he could control it.

Ymir bit her lip. "I told you, I've failed my people before. The last god to steal the Gulltop from me kicked the gods out of Asgard."

My eyes went wide. "Baldr had control over the Gull-top? How did you get it back from him?"

Her gaze darkened. "With enough sacrifice, anything is possible."

Now I understood the weight of guilt Ymir carried around with her. It wasn't just the creation of the Jotun that rested on her shoulders, but the reason the Surtr were nearly an extinct race. Their cavernous city of Jotunheim held only a mere few hundred Surtr. Jotun like the Huldra numbered in the thousands.

"I see," I said. "So, if we're to keep control of the Gull-top, we need someone to manually release the lava." Why did it have to be Will. I would have offered myself, but if anything happened to me, there'd be no one to stop Ragnarök or my insane brother. Ymir couldn't do it. I needed her to run the Gulltop. I certainly couldn't ask any of the other Surtr to give their lives so that Will might live.

There was one last weapon in my arsenal. The Yggdrasil fruit still in my pouch.

The concentration of raw life lived underneath its soft flesh. Perhaps if I got him to take a bite before he sacrificed himself… I could still save him.

I glanced at Ymir. "I have an idea, but you're not going to like it."

W e dialed in the time stamp to just a few moments after I began my call with Baldr. Traveling through time with the Gulltop wasn't any easier the second round and my screams echoed through time and space as we ripped through the natural world and followed the threads to where I needed to go.

My feet met the smooth, warm stone of Jotunheim and Ymir joined me at the tunnel's entrance to the hologram room. We'd stop Will before he ran out.

"Are you sure about this?" Ymir asked.

I'd explained my plan to her in its entirety, but I couldn't be sure if it would work. Yggdrasil's fruit traveled with me and I wouldn't be able to restore it after its use.

I nodded and spread my feet. "I'm sure."

Baldr's mocking voice echoed through the corridor and I scraped my fingernails against my palm. Will came barreling into us a moment later, nearly plowing us over on his way to the Gulltop.

He balked at me. "Val?" He looked back at the room, the dark silhouette behind the screen being my past self, then he looked back at me. "What is going on?"

I held both hands. "There isn't much time to explain, but you're on your way to unlock the Gulltop. It worked."

His shoulders relaxed. "Good." Then his jaw flexed. "If you've come to try and stop me, you're wasting your time. This is the only way you can fight Ragnarök and you know it."

I nodded. "I'm not trying to stop you. I think you're brave, stupid, and heroic, and you're right." I pulled the golden fruit from my pouch and offered it to him. "But you don't have to die."

He stared at it. "You need that."

I shook my head. "No. This is why I took it in the first place. It was all to save you."

He flinched, but reached out and ran his fingers over mine as he took the fruit. He didn't let go of me. The rainbow specks glimmered, hope flickering in the backs of eyes that should have been chestnut brown and warm. "I'm not worthy of all that you do for me."

I pushed the fruit at him. "Just take it. We don't have much time."

I slipped my fingers away from his and he lifted the fruit to his mouth. The golden skin glowed against his lips… then he took a bite.

Light exploded and Ymir dashed behind me to avoid the worst of the blow. I flared my wings to protect her. I didn't know what the fruit of Yggdrasil would do. All I knew was that it was power and raw life. It would give Will a chance against the lava that would come bearing down on him when he went to free the Gulltop.

He handed the fruit back to me with a small piece missing. He'd barely taken a bite and tiny teeth marks glowed around the wounded fruit. I lifted it again, about to tell him that he should eat the whole thing, but he dashed around me, faster than he should have been.

Gold blurred through the corridors, and then Will was gone.

Time distorted and pain snapped through my spine.

"You did it," Ymir breathed. "You changed the timeline."

I clenched my fists against the fresh waves of pain as I struggled to stay in one piece. It felt as if tiny claws raked against the inside of my ribcage, threatening to tear me apart. "What'll happen to us?" I was the product of my timeline. Would I simply cease to exist?

I looked too Ymir, but she blurred. My vision distorted as dizziness swept over me, and then my body began to disintegrate. Bits of ash ran down my fingers and burning agony swept through me.

I'd been through this before. This was how I'd felt when the Einherjar sent me to earth. When I'd shed my Immortal skin in favor of a mortal one. Except, this time I wasn't getting a human body. I was merging with my Immortal self in this new present.

I blinked a few times, readjusting as I found myself on the platform with the screen around me gone black. Baldr had just informed me that I was a god in my own right, capable of commanding Ragnarök and feeding off of its power. I could give life where I'd taken it, the trait of any god. Life was like any other energy in the universe. It could never be destroyed... only transformed.

When Wills screams rocked my body and the caverns trembled, I ran after him just like I had before. When I slammed into Mr. Jefferson, he tried to tell me about Will, but I didn't need to hear it this time. I knew exactly where to go.

I sped down the halls and found the chamber with lava freshly drained and the Gulltop lopsided, ready for me once again.

But this time Will had survived the onslaught. His blackened body trembled on the edge of one of the massive drains. I ran through the broken diamond wall and to his side. Had I saved him, only to watch him suffer?

He lifted a hand and tried to speak. No words came out.

"Will?" I asked, my voice breaking.

His hand fell to the black rune across my knuckles, and then I knew what I had to do.

———

I absorbed the remains of Will's soul, but I didn't draw him into myself like I had before. This time I held him in one piece and carried him as carefully as a breakable porcelain statue in the heart of my mind.

I opened a portal through space and time, using the lasting power of Will's sacrifice to fuel the trick. I only needed a small jump. I didn't need the Bifrost to step between the folds of space, not when I had the fuel.

I only used a sliver for the small step to the surface of Muspelheim. I walked out into the center of the great city of Valkyries. Golden spires towered all around me and a shocked group of traitors stared back at me.

Skuld... and my undead sisters.

They came at me in a wave of snarls and teeth. That's exactly what I wanted. Now that I knew what I was capable of, I had no qualms about feeding on the tattered remains of their souls.

I drew in the darkness and the first wave fell around me in a pile of ash. The rest of the army stopped in their tracks, halting at the dusty circle.

I ignored them while they cursed and snarled. They were all made of grief and torment and they had no concept of right or wrong. A moment ago, I was their enemy, but now that I'd decimated their comrades, I was something to be feared.

The sacrifice of shadow swirled in the air and I did something I'd only done once before. I opened up to it. Without even knowing what I was doing, I'd created bodies before. At the time, they'd remained empty shells, decoys to throw at the bottom of the lake and get the humans off our trail.

This time I recreated Will's flesh down to the finest detail. I imagined how he was before all of this. He was a swimmer, lean and strong, but with the growing form of a human that would eventually age and die. I hated the thought of Will dying, but that was the cycle of life and how it was meant to be. He would live a full life, and then he would be free to return to Yggdrasil.

I settled a forcefield around us to keep out the worst of the radiation and heat while I did my work. I wasn't going to give him the curse of a Valiant's form. He'd never wanted Immortality. Will's flesh formed from the ash, swirling and writhing until it formed an arm, then a leg, then the slow embodiment that was the mortal shell to his soul.

His spirit rested inside my mind and carefully I pulled it out and pushed it into the new body I'd formed. It wasn't that I'd created life, but I felt a sense of accomplishment and awe when he drew in a deep breath, the first in his new body.

He stood, and I'd expected him to be shaky as a newborn. Instead his thighs flexed and his muscular arms wrapped around me, embracing me as he drew in another breath.

His low voice sounded like music against my ears. "Val. I'm alive."

FULL CIRCLE

I was so amazingly happy in that moment that I nearly forgot there was an army of Skuld and undead Valkyries flanking us. Finally, one arrived that wasn't afraid of me.

Sam snarled and marched up to us. She glowed with the fires of Muspelheim, but she wasn't like I remembered her. She jerked in ungraceful movements as if her muscles were too stiff and flesh rotted off her bones, only for the wound to burn with cinders and knit back together. I realized that it was the power of Ragnarök that kept her alive.

"Sam?" I asked, wondering if I could reason with her.

She growled a low, guttural sound that wasn't even close to a word.

"I don't think that's Sam anymore," Will whispered as he covered himself, realizing that he was naked. "Good thing, or she'd be making fun of me right now. Naked in the middle of a Valkyrie city surrounded by ghosts. Talk about nightmares."

I waved him into silence. "Just be grateful you're alive."

Sam stalked us in a slow circle, looking as if she were debating the best way to hack into my skull and eat my brains.

I didn't have time for this. I'd saved Will, but now I needed to save Tyler, the Einherjar, and everyone inside of it. I glanced up at the haze of red clouds that blotted out the sky. The Einherjar was up there, somewhere, and I could only hope that Tyler had been able to hold on. If he'd fallen, I wasn't sure if even the Gulltop could save him while he'd been in the middle of distorting the space-time web in order for me to get to Muspelheim.

"Get out of my way," I barked, not caring anymore if this thing that impersonated Sam could understand me. I summoned my spear in a flash of heat and pointed it at her. She snarled at it. "I'm like Baldr. If you serve him because he can control Ragnarök, then you should serve me."

To my surprise, Sam grinned as if I'd said something hilarious. The edge of her lip lifted, revealing teeth and bone.

That's when I felt it. A heartbeat thrummed through my body and nausea made me buckle over.

"You're not ready," Sam whispered, the words barely audible through the garble of her broken vocal cords.

Will steadied me, but hissed as the raw heat of my flesh left his skin blistered. "What's she talking about? Val? What's wrong?"

It felt like I'd eaten something bad, then multiplied that feeling by a thousand. Baldr had opened my eyes that I could feed on the darkness... but then I realized, wasn't that exactly what the Norn did?

Shadows sprouted across my arms like weeds bursting through my flesh and I cried out. I gathered a fistful of the sprouts and ripped them from my body. There was no way I was going to get this far and turn into a Norn!

"Not ready," Sam hissed again. She cocked her head to the side as if listening, then nodded. "He sends you home."

I didn't have time to ask who "he" was. The glittering

black fingers of Ragnarök that lingered on the horizon zeroed in on the city and dove down straight for us.

I held my forcefield tight. I wasn't going to let it be broken and the inhospitable atmosphere rip Will up from the inside. I'd worked so hard to get him back into a mortal body. I wasn't going to let anything take that away, not even Ragnarök.

But the fingers weren't trying to destroy us. Darkness enveloped the sphere I held around us until only my internal flame illuminated our surroundings. I knelt and held onto Will. Nausea and pain continued to streak through me, but Ragnarök's presence was... actually soothing.

I felt the slip of time and space underneath us shift, then we were falling, and even though I should have been terrified, I held onto Will's hand, and he held onto mine. No matter what happened, we were together.

*R*agnarök spit us out onto a dusty trail in the middle of a forest that looked suspiciously reminiscent of Central Park.

When the darkness retreated, leaving us only with silver moonlight filtering through the trees, I heard laughter in the distance.

Human laughter.

Still holding onto Will, I slowly stood. My wings flared out of instinct to keep me balanced.

I couldn't believe it. We were back on Earth.

Will released a long breath. "Well, that was unexpected."

I released him as I took a few steps and then paused. "Yeah." I tilted my head and listened, but there was no sound of Baldr's laughter or any sign that this was a trick. "Why would he send us back to earth? He totally had us." And whatever he'd done, he'd soothed the nausea winding in my stomach that would have turned me into a Norn.

"Who?" Will asked.

I turned and almost laughed. He was still naked. I blushed and looked away. "Uh, Will."

He looked down. "Oh, crap." He covered himself. "Well aren't we the pair. A naked dude with a Valkyrie. We're not going to stand out at all."

Leaves rustled and glittered, and then I heard another kind of laugh. The tinkering joy of a Huldra. I ignored the fluttering of my heart hoping that it would be Jules. The unwanted image of her lifeless on the ground shoved itself to the front of my mind.

Brushing aside the painful memories, I followed the trail of glitter and motioned for Will to follow. One of Dalia's Huldra, whether they could be trusted or not, was a better guide than hoping I could find my way out on my own. To my relief, the flutter of the leaves led us straight to the luxury condo we'd stayed in what seemed like a lifetime ago.

The door buzzed at my touch, opening and allowing us in.

"What do you think?" I asked when we entered into the familiar room. The fireplace was just as I remembered it, surrounded by a jumble of pillows enticing for a group to just sit and talk. My heart yearned for those days when it'd been all of us. Tyler, Will, and Jules. I hadn't appreciated having them all together, but now I missed it.

Will closed the door behind us. "I think Dalia realizes she chose the wrong side."

I hummed thoughtfully and flexed my wings, grateful

to finally be able to properly stretch them. I wouldn't be able to go for a leisure flight around here, not without activating Thor as it wiped thousands of human minds after being spotted. Even if my mother wasn't around to enforce it, the A.I. program would still keep tabs, especially during Ragnarök. The last thing my mother needed was for one of her worlds to go on full-out panic during the end of the world. That would only feed Ragnarök more and make it more difficult to imprison.

"If Dalia has really switched sides, then I want to talk to her," I said.

I turned when there was no response, finding Will had already disappeared down the hall. All I saw was the flash of a handsome male buttocks before he disappeared into a room. I grinned, shamelessly filing that memory away for when I was feeling down.

Will returned shortly in customary jeans and a loose fitting Tee. He smiled his warm, sensual smile. "Why're you looking at me like that?"

Happiness bubbled out of me like a fountain and I had to keep my emotions in, lest they seep out as flame and singe the carpet. After everything we'd been through, Will was right here in front of me, mortal, and free of the Norn's curse.

It wasn't over, not by a long-shot. Ragnarök was still out there and once it was done with Muspelheim, I knew Baldr would have no qualms about letting it destroy this world. I didn't want to turn into a Norn myself, and until I figured out how to feed on darkness without that happening, Baldr and Ragnarök were still my greatest threat.

"I'm just glad you are finally human again," I said. Effortlessly I moved to squeeze his arm, but he flinched the instant I grazed his skin. "Oh, sorry."

His mood turned sour. "When I imagined getting my human body back, I didn't expect you to be in your Valkyrie form. I can't even touch you." He ghosted his fingers over my arm, then made a fist. "Do you think you can do for yourself what you did for me?"

I slowly shook my head. "Not any time soon. You saw what happened. When I fed on darkness, I almost became…" My words drifted. I couldn't say it out loud.

He grimaced and slumped into the sofa across from the fireplace. "You would become like my mother."

I curled up on the floor and hugged a pillow to my

chest, releasing it when it began to smolder. With a sigh, I released the heat that wanted to get out and directed it to the fireplace. Long dead logs engulfed in a flame that burst to life.

I'd never imagined my future with Will to be anything permanent. But now that I was here, living this new present with him, I wasn't sure what was going to happen next.

COMING OUT OF THE CLOSET

I insisted that Will go to bed, but he refused to leave me alone. I wasn't going to leave the fireplace. My emotions were a wreck and the metal grate full of flame was the only safe spot I could release the embers dying to get out of me. I wasn't on Muspelheim anymore and I had so much pent-up energy inside of me. I thought of Elena and Michael. She'd lost her wings, but not the flame that lived in her heart. She'd become something closer to human than I certainly was. I recalled her sitting on the couch sipping tea.

I glanced through the room, sweeping my gaze over a sleeping Will on the couch. Even if he'd refused to leave me, he still had slipped into unconsciousness. Coming back from the dead must have been tiring.

I wandered through the condo and looked for a phone, then laughed. Elena was probably halfway across the world right now. I didn't even know her number.

A low hum brought me out of my thoughts and I frowned. Tilting my head, I heard it again, a buzz that didn't sound mechanical. I followed it into one of the bedrooms. It was coming from the closet.

I was glad the knobs were metal. They wouldn't disintegrate under my touch. I grabbed it and yanked it open, not sure what I was going to find inside.

Instead of a walk-in closet filled with clothes, a familiar room appeared, one with telescopes and a particular immortal with a golden grill for a smile.

"Well, hello dear. Aren't you a sight for sore eyes?"

I'd wanted to speak to Dalia, but this was not how I'd imagined it. "Did you seriously just use the Bifrost to teleport to my bedroom?"

Dalia held up a finger. "Actually, it's my bedroom. You're only borrowing it."

Glowering, I stepped inside. Time and space slipped

over me like a blanket as I entered the pocket realm of the Bifrost.

"What do you want?" I snapped.

She grinned. "I want what I've always wanted. I'm a simple creature."

She motioned for me to sit across from her desk and I glowered before yanking the seat out and sitting on it. I allowed the heat of Muspelheim to billow from my body, but the chair stood up under the onslaught. I draped my wings over the back and a shower of embers flew across the ground. It didn't surprise me that the Bifrost was Valkyrie-proof. "And what is it that you want?" I asked. "Power?"

She laughed. "Hardly, dear." She leaned onto her elbows and sighed. "I just want a place my children can be free. Is that too much to ask?"

I narrowed my eyes. The Bifrost shook, sending the telescopes clinking against one another. "What's that all about?" I asked.

She leaned back in her chair and propped her boots up on the desk. "Just Baldr getting a little fussy that I'm talking to you. He thought he was so clever sending you to earth." She winked. "He doesn't want you dead, or turned into a Norn. He wants you to join him."

I crossed my arms. "Well that's not going to happen."

"And I tried to tell him that," she said with a nod. "But you know how he is. He thinks everyone will bow down and worship at his feet." She rolled her eyes. "I'm quite grateful he's no longer at the top of the food chain. Even if he had agreed to spare the Heimdall line, it almost would have been worth extinction to slap him across the face."

A smirk came to my lips and I tried to douse the amusement Dalia always managed to awaken in me. She was likable, but she was dangerous. I wouldn't forget who I was dealing with. "You know, I remember outside your restaurant there were statues of the gods. My memory isn't so good. Who was the fourth one? Was it Baldr?" Technically, after I'd seen what he could do, he was a god by definition. Converting energy and bringing life into being was the only requirement. Dalia, Odin, and Freya had their own strengths that accomplished that task, but Baldr and I, we were wrong. He didn't deserve a statue.

She smiled. "You think I'd have a statue of that creep?"

She slammed her hand on the desk and bellowed a laugh. "Hilarious!"

I frowned. "Then who is it?"

Her mood turned somber. "You really don't remember, do you?"

Now I was starting to get impatient. Another boom rocked the Bifrost, but I ignored it. Let Baldr have his little tantrum. "No, I don't."

Her smile mixed with her usual sarcasm and a hint of mournful sadness. "The fourth god is an ideal, a leader among us who doesn't exist yet." She pulled out her phone and shoved it across the desk. "Here. Take a look."

I leaned over and peered at the image that displayed her restaurant. It was an ad online depicting "food to die for," which was a horrible pun. But then I spotted the row of statues and frowned. The last one was a man covered in runes. Hair swept back and even through the stone gaze, I could sense the mischief behind it. "That's Tyler," I said. "You think your son is a god?"

She laughed. "You know, I had that statue built before he was even born." She took the phone back and smiled at the image. "Perhaps one of my visions saw him and was hopeful." A click sounded as she locked the phone's screen and returned the device back to her pocket. "Or perhaps, Tyler will be the one to save us all."

***

The idea of Tyler coming to my rescue wasn't so far-fetched. He'd done exactly that for me a thousand times. Every rune he bore on his body was a scar of sin he took so that I didn't have to. "So how does he do it?" I asked, half-fascinated and half-mortified. "How does he feed on a soul without turning into something like a Norn?"

I'd only known Valkyries to be able to manipulate the energy of souls, but the Heimdall line was a unique case. They acted as servants to the gods and each had their own skills. I'd met a few of Tyler's brothers on occasion. Now that my memories were returning, I recalled they didn't appreciate one of their own playing bodyguard to a Valkyrie that only put him further at risk. If he gave in to the darkness because of me, he'd turn into something worse than a Norn.

"Tyler is strong," Dalia said, pride dripping from her

voice as she swayed her chair back. "As are all of my sons. We're a form of the Jotun, but when I discovered how to manipulate energy and create life, that's when I became a god and the Heimdall became a new race. The Bifrost was given to me by Ymir herself to safeguard. That was back when she trusted me, of course."

I nodded. "Right." Now that I thought about it, Tyler had gone out of his way to make sure I hadn't seen that fourth statue. I frowned. "What does Tyler think of this?"

Her golden teeth flashed as she laughed. She twirled one of her telescopes across her fingers. "He's always been arrogant, but the idea of being a god appalls him. He'd rather 'eat embers,' as he says."

A smile twitched at my mouth at Tyler's phrase. He loved to tell mouthy Valkyries to eat their own embers.

Warmth radiated down my spine as I thought about the Einherjar. "So the alliance with Freya, that was to feed Tyler the souls he needs as one of the Heimdall."

Dalia's smile faded. "He told you?"

I shrugged. "He tried to, but I figured it out. Are all the Heimdall soul-sucking monsters?"

The room darkened and another boom shook the Bifrost, but I had a feeling it wasn't Baldr this time. "My son is no monster."

"No," I agreed. "He was just unfortunate enough to inherit the family trait."

Dalia all but launched at me across the desk. She grabbed a telescope and chucked it at my face. I dodged just in time to catch another in my wing. "You will speak of my son with respect!"

I held up my hands in surrender. The Bifrost was a small enough room as it was without an enraged mother throwing telescopes at me. I rubbed my wing. "Fine, all right." I shook the appendage and worked out the bruise. "Tyler is trapped on the Einherjar, did you know that? Baldr is attacking him and everyone on board." I knew why Baldr didn't want the Einherjar to survive. It was the one force in the universe that held the power—and the people—capable of stopping him. With the strengths of all the gods combined, there was a chance to do the impossible and stop Ragnarök itself. No Ragnarök, no darkness, and no Baldr.

"Why do you think I'm helping you?" she snapped and slammed another telescope on the desk instead of throwing it at me. The lens shattered and glass fell across the desk. "I'm the caretaker of the Bifrost and I can see everything that transpires within a hundred miles of my vicinity. I saw the Skuld and the Valkyrie head straight for him and that human of yours." Her lower lip quivered before she sank her teeth into it. "Do you know how helpless it feels to have the power of space and time at your grasp, but to be unable to help your own son when darkness befalls him?"

I shrank my wings to my back. I knew exactly what it felt like to be unable to help those you loved. "Darkness haunts me," I admitted. "I want this all to end."

She straightened. "Darkness doesn't have to haunt you, my dear. As a Heimdall, I for one know how to turn it into a strength."

KINDRED SOULS

*L*essons from Dalia, the goddess of the Bifrost, and a gangster who ruled New York, as well as few select planetary provinces—from her own testimony—led me to believe that we had a fighting chance against Baldr. There was one last thing I needed to stop him, and that was to get Tyler to admit he was a god.

He was going to love that.

I found Will sitting on the edge of the couch when I arrived. He stared into the dying flames and looked pensive with his hands folded as he rested his elbows on his knees. When my wings sent the fire flaring back to life, he finally glanced at me.

"You were gone," he said, his voice raw from either sleep or emotion, I couldn't tell.

I bit my lip. "Yeah, sorry. Dalia paid me a visit."

He frowned. "You should have called for me. We're supposed to be in this together."

I swept past him, careful not to brush my feathers against his skin, and pulled the drapes aside. I frowned when the fabric blackened under my touch.

Outside, the morning sun cast cheery rays onto an emerald forest that spanned out in a long line between the metallic spires of civilization. Modern sky rises looked almost out of place next to the trees and greenery. "I meant to tell you that I met your mother in Scandinavia."

Will shot to his feet. "What?"

I leaned so close to the glass that the heat of my breath fogged it. "I tried to stop her from dedicating you to the gods."

He came to my side and moved as if to touch me, then curled his fingers away. "When you used the Gulltop, you gave me the Yggdrasil fruit. I wondered what could have happened that you'd allow me to go through with sacrificing myself, even if you knew you could bring me back. But to go back to my first life..." I saw the pain in his eyes. He considered it a betrayal to even think about altering the timeline so that we would have never met.

"She was different, back then. You were sick, and you had a sister who had died before you." The truth spilled out of me like a wave and tears sizzled in my eyes. "I couldn't stop her from dedicating you. I thought that if I did, none of this would happen, and you could have lived a normal human life like you were supposed to." I sniffled and looked at the length of him. He was perfect, just the way he was, but I could sense the darkness running through his veins. I'd caused him so much suffering. Even now, wisps of torment glittered across his skin. "Why are you in so much pain?"

He cornered me against the wall and slammed his fist against it. "Because, Val, I can't touch you. I can't make you stop grieving this life that you wanted for me. I can't do anything."

Helpless. I understood what Dalia meant now, how it felt to see everything that you wanted to fix and being powerless to do anything about it. I matched Will's gaze, relaxing under the familiar chestnut calm of his mortality. "You know," he continued, "when I first realized how I felt about you, it wasn't because I felt a surge of passion or a wave of joy. It was the thought of being without you wrecking my insides until I felt sick. Being apart from you torments me, but I ignore it. I do what I think is right."

He spread his fingers out against the wall and leaned as close as he could. The heat sizzled off my skin and turned his skin pink. His lips hovered over mine and I knew he wanted to crush into me, speak to me with his body when words wouldn't work anymore. But I was a Valkyrie, and he was human. We could never be together and make it work.

His mouth parted, his words crushing me instead. "That's not love, Val. That's duty."

With the sting of his rejection hanging in the air, he shoved off the wall and stormed out of the room. The door closed behind him. He didn't slam it. He simply closed it, and I'd never felt anything so final in all my life.

I expected Will to come home at least by nightfall. I rummaged through the refrigerator and found it stocked with sodas. In the freezer were plenty of dinners to tide a single human over as long as we needed. Until I figured out how to rescue

Tyler, I had no plans on resuming my mortal form, as much as I missed frozen spaghetti.

A part of me never wanted to feel what it was to be human again. It was better this way. If Will could touch me, then I'd forget everything we'd just said to each other. I didn't want to forget.

Even though I'd poured myself a carbonated drink and watched the ice swim around in the glass, I didn't sip. The moment I touched it the ice would melt and the soda would turn into a bubbling frothy mess. I knew that Elena had somehow managed to control her heat, but she'd spent lifetimes on earth acclimating to this world. I didn't have that kind of time.

When Will finally returned, I snapped my head up and blinked at the doorway. He wasn't alone.

I'd just been thinking of the powerful Valkyrie with torn wings, and there she was, smiling at me until I almost didn't recognize her. I'd never seen Elena smile like that, like she was truly happy.

Then I saw why. Behind her stepped out a man and he slipped an arm around her waist before giving her a kiss on the cheek. "Well would you look at that. This guy wasn't nuts after all."

I nearly swallowed my tongue. "...Michael?"

*A*pparently our little venture through time and space had a little consequence of twenty years passing us by. Ragnarök had such weight and mass, we'd slowed down while the rest of the world had kept spinning. It boggled my mind that even without the Gulltop, I still had to worry about slipping through time.

Michael hadn't stopped grinning. Even though he wore a different body, I'd recognize that soul anywhere. He'd once been a vegetable and a mind trapped in a loop of permanent nightmare... but something had changed.

That's when I had enough sense to check my leathers. "Where's the fruit of Yggdrasil?" I snapped.

Will plucked it from his jacket and handed it back to me. "About burned off my hand trying to get that."

Rage turned my vision red and Elena stepped between me and Will. "Calm down, sweetie. Will just did a good thing."

I allowed her to drag me away to the kitchen. It

seemed to be where humans liked to talk and Elena had been around them long enough to adopt their quirks. Two male voices hummed in the background.

"He stole it," I complained as I sat onto a chair. It creaked with warning under me, but I didn't care if it burned to pieces. "He let me think he wanted to kiss me, and then he just stole it."

Elena smirked, which didn't help my mood. "Sweetie, that boy wants to kiss you more than anyone I've seen. I'm sure he can multitask."

I narrowed my eyes, but the heat drained from me, leaving a low warmth in my chest. "So, how did he find you?" I shifted uncomfortably in my chair. "Don't get me wrong. I'm happy for you. You finally have Michael back."

She beamed. "It's just, it's incredible. I never imagined I'd get to talk to him and he'd know who I was." She reached out and took my hand. I flinched, but then relaxed when I realized she couldn't get burned. She was just as much a Valkyrie as I was. "Will went to Dalia's restaurant and asked for her help to find us. Dalia keeps tabs on all Immortals, especially those like myself."

I raised an eyebrow. "So, there are more out there like

Michael?" Perhaps it wasn't so uncommon to break the first law of the Valkyrie.

She nodded. "Yes, and with your help, we can find them and help them like Will helped Michael. It's incredible."

I untangled my fingers from hers and pulled the fruit from my pouch. A slice was missing now, the wound next to the teeth-mark where Will had taken his bite. "Do you know what this is?" I asked.

She folded her hands. "I believe I do. What I don't know is how you got your hands on it."

I tucked it back into my pouch. "I'm a Frigg, remember?"

Her eyes went wide. "You must be a powerful one if you can travel all the way to Yggdrasil and make it back alive."

I told her the whole story, not leaving out the bit that I didn't think I could ever travel to Yggdrasil again. I got the one shot—and we had the one piece of fruit. I couldn't just go squandering it on lost souls, as much as I wanted to.

Elena opened her mouth to protest, but then the table's centerpiece, a vase with a wilted rose, lifted on its own and floated in midair. I stared at it. "Are you doing that?"

She shook her head slowly from side-to-side.

The vase crashed to the table, breaking into splintered pieces and tossing the contents to the ground. I jumped when Michael cleared his throat.

Will grinned. "Turns out Michael has a little secret."

Elena shot to her feet. "You have telekinesis?"

Michael blew her a kiss and she flinched, her hand flinging up to her face. By the look of shock, I suspected he'd just made sure she'd felt that. "You bet I do, and we're going to kick some serious Norn butt. It's about time the tables have turned."

---

*M*ichael's powers were only the start of the weirdness. What worried me the most was that Will hadn't seemed surprised by Michael's inhuman ability.

When I tried to talk to him about it, he told me that he had to find the others. When I asked him what he meant, he sputtered and said Dalia had told him—but had she?

I paid the Heimdall a visit myself, which revealed that there were three other cases of Valkyries who were exiled and still watched over their charges. Will ventured out, determined to find each one.

Still looking like a freak who'd just walked out of a comic convention, I couldn't leave the condo. I'd never felt so confined in all my life, not even when I'd spent five years training in the caverns of Jotunheim.

Each time Will returned, Yggdrasil's fruit had a little bit less power, and our household grew until everywhere I turned was a friendly face.

The other Valkyries looked similar to Elena. Freya had ripped off their wings and banished them to earth. I would have expected them to hold some sort of resentment against me. I still had my wings even though I'd broken the first law of the Valkyrie, but they weren't like my sisters. They were loving and kind and quick to embrace me as one of their own. That just made everything worse.

The new couples were so amazingly happy to finally be together that their bliss gave no room for sorrow.

They'd experienced the horror of Elena and Michael's same situation for lifetimes.

Iris and Paul. They'd been the closest and easiest to find. Dalia had taken Will off to Windsor, one of the provinces of Canada to pick them up. Iris mesmerized me with the way her eyes changed. One green and one a ruby red. Even though she was ancient, she had the body of a fit, but mature thirty-year-old and she claimed she was becoming more human every day. She wanted to age, and I wondered if she was starting to succeed. Most Valkyries looked to be around sixteen to twenty. Her goal had always been to embrace mortality so that one day, she could find a way to free Paul from his torment and join him in the bliss of Yggdrasil. It was a novel concept, but I didn't have the heart to tell her that even if she found a way to become truly mortal, her soul would always belong to Muspelheim.

Nina and Henry. They took Dalia a few tries to locate, as they were buried in the deep lush of the Amazon. Nina prowled like a wild animal, playfully snapping at anyone who dared venture too close to Henry. He encouraged the primal behavior, petting her as if she were a cat. What made her stand out the most was that her eyes weren't red at all, but an aquamarine blue that matched her exotic appearance.

Helena and Daniel. Now they were an even odder pair. Helena sat straight with her hands folded over her knee as she sat across from Daniel. They both reeked of sophistication and wealth. As seemed customary, they challenged each other with a game of poker that no one else was allowed to play. Helena took an elegant finger and slid a chip across the table. Straight out of Vegas, she'd made sure that Daniel had every luxury. What had started as a dancer gig where even a Valkyrie might fit in had turned into a long-term game where she played backdoor poker games and lost just enough hands not to get thrown out of the house.

They were the latest addition to our growing cluster of weirdos, and now that it was all said and done, only a single sliver of Yggdrasil's fruit remained.

Will had taken me aside to return it to me. We'd hardly spoken these last few days while he'd been out on his "field trips."

He held out what was left of the precious fruit. Having saved the final soul on Dalia's list, I suppose he thought he had no use for it anymore. He grimaced, having the nerve to look apologetic that perhaps he'd squeezed all the use out of it.

I snatched the core back from him. I couldn't hold it in anymore. The words spilled out of me on their own as rage glimmered in the backs of my eyes, tingeing my vision red. "I know I'm supposed to understand, or whatever, but I went all the way to Yggdrasil to get this fruit for *you*, not anybody else. I'm not some kind of charity. And not to sound selfish about it, but we still have Ragnarök to worry about." I hadn't told him, but I'd felt its icy fingers growing ever closer to this world. Once it drained Muspelheim dry, there'd be nothing to hold it back. Not even Baldr—no matter how pompous and arrogant he thought he was—could stop a force like that from devouring entire worlds. "None of this matters if we all die."

Will crossed his arms and leaned against the wall. Normally he would have immediately sniped back at me, but he was exhausted, even if he wouldn't admit it. Dark circles under his eyes betrayed how little he'd slept while he'd been off playing hero. Being human again took its toll and as much as he pretended he could keep up, he couldn't fool me.

"Just look at them, Val," he said, his voice gravely, but stern.

I followed his gaze through the thin glass that separated us from the rest of the living room where the odd matchup of Valkyrie and human pairs seemed to all get along. The Valkyries took turns lighting the wood while Nina doused the flames with water, just to see if they could still burn it. The contents of the fireplace sizzled with protest and Nina squealed with delight when she managed to snuff it out. Even though smoke billowed into the room, Henry smiled at her as if she were the most adorable thing in the world.

My new housemates had been cooped up in this condo nearly as long as I had been, but they didn't seem to mind. Even if the other Valkyries had learned how to contain the majority of the supernatural heat in their bodies, they certainly couldn't pass for human. Metallic skin and gorgeous glowing eyes made them stand out, as well as their supernatural grace and beauty that came with being one of Freya's daughters.

"Yes, they seem happy," I admitted, although the edge of my voice made it clear that was irrelevant to this conversation.

Will narrowed his eyes. "Isn't that enough? If you've learned anything from me, it's that I believe in the power of the present."

He was starting to get on my nerves, and he knew it. "News flash," I snapped, "I'm a Frigg. I live in the constant flow of time and space. There is more to the universe than the present. Without the future, you have nothing, and I intend to make sure there's a future for all of us if I can help it."

Will frowned. "I know you're angry."

I tossed the fruit to the ground. It didn't bounce like I'd expect fruit to do. Instead it ricocheted and sent a crack through the tiles. I glanced at the Valkyries and their men and found them watching us now. "I'm not angry. I'm pissed."

Will knelt and picked up the core. His fingers turned pink at its raw heat before he wrapped it in a towel. "I'm sorry I used so much of it. It's just, when I heard there were others like me—"

"It's not about the fruit," I snapped, then lowered my voice, hoping the others couldn't hear me. "I just." I looked down at my hands. The perfectly smooth skin glimmered as embers blazed through my veins. "I don't get why things are like this between us now." I met his gaze, hating how pathetic I sounded. "Is it because you can't touch me?"

He sighed. "I know it's hard. We both misinterpreted

what we are to one another."

"*Misinterpreted?*" I squeaked.

"Just hear me out, Val. We thought we were soulmates, that we completed each other just because it hurt so much to be apart, but ever since I took a bite of that fruit…"

My eyes widened. "You lost your feelings for me."

He wouldn't meet my gaze. "I don't think it's that I lost something." His eyes shot up and those chestnut irises met mine, full of hope and longing, but this time he wasn't longing for me. "Our attraction to one other, it's there, I won't deny that." He moved so that he backed me against the glass. My feathers crunched against my back, but I didn't complain as he pressed a hand and leaned so that our breaths mingled. "You're my Valkyrie. I'm your soul. That's our bond to one another, and when you gave me what the Norn took away, you gave me back my freedom."

Pain made my vision blur. I couldn't listen to Will talk this way as if a bite from some fruit could destroy his feelings for me. "Then what about them?" I asked, not caring anymore how my voice grated with the thousand tiny daggers that plunged through my bruised heart.

He watched them and a low murmur of voices resumed as they pretended not to be dying to know what we were talking about. Daniel cheered, having won his latest hand against his mate. "Their bonds are too strong. Those humans have been reborn so many times with nothing but their Valkyrie to guide them that they don't know any other way of life. I won't deny it's something akin to love." He turned to me and stroked away my hair, his skin just far enough away from mine so as not to get burned. "The difference is, Val, your heart doesn't belong to me. It never did."

My stomach twisted and I clutched at it. I wanted to tell him that he was wrong, that I didn't love Tyler, but for some reason my voice wouldn't dare utter those words aloud. "I don't get it," I whispered. "They don't burn anyone who tries to touch them." I met his gaze. "Yet you and I, we burn each other until one of us turns to ash."

He huffed a laugh and I hated how sexy it was. "After a few centuries, I'm sure even a Valkyrie can learn to contain her passion, hide who she is and pretend." He dared to press a kiss against my hair, pulling away with a hiss. "But not you, Val. Never forget who you are."

ALLIES

*D*alia surprised all of us by showing up at our doorstep with a bedazzled telescope in one hand and a giant bottle of wine in the other. She gave me a golden smile as I stood there like an idiot. "Do you always answer the door looking like that?" she asked, her grin only growing wider.

I flared my wings, reluctant to admit perhaps it was pretty stupid to be answering the door, but with so much going on, I forgot that I wasn't human. "That's what Grimhildr is for," I muttered and moved aside so that she could enter. "What brings you here, on foot no less? My closet not good enough for you anymore?"

She laughed. "Ah, don't sound so sour, dear. It's not often that I leave the comfort of the Bifrost. Take honor where honor is due."

"Dali!" Nina screeched and ran on all fours before sweeping the small woman up in her arms.

"You two… know each other?" I asked as I shut the door, more than a little bewildered. "What's an outcast and a Heimdall got in common?" I grinned, because that sounded like the start to a terrible joke.

Henry followed his mate and laughed. "Well I'll be damned, it's the goddess herself."

Dalia gave him a fond smile, shoving the bottle of wine into my chest before giving his cheek a pinch. "It's a downright miracle. I can't believe it." She waved in welcome as the rest of the couples entered the room. "Iris and Paul," she said, marveling. "Helena and Daniel." She swept across the room and gave each of them a kiss.

Will stood in the doorway and smirked. "You should just tell her, Dalia, before Val turns this place into an inferno."

I realized that the wine I was holding was starting to boil. Dalia frowned. "Well that's unfortunate, dear. I do prefer my wine chilled."

"Would you care to tell me how you all know each other?"

Dalia smiled. "You know, the way your mother treated her daughters who broke one of her precious laws that she herself couldn't even uphold always baffled me. I took it upon myself to care for them and help them find their mates during the recycle process."

Paul, Henry, and Daniel collectively shivered at the term. Paul gripped his mate's arm. "Tell her not to call it that. She makes it sound less horrendous than it was."

Daniel straightened his bowtie, and it was the only sign that he'd been fazed. "Agreed. You shall never use that term in our presence again."

Dalia rolled her eyes and shoved her way past them. "Fine. But enough chit-chat. I've come here on important business."

Curious, we followed her to the living room. The hearth with flames that never died—not with four Valkyries in the room—illuminated the jeweled telescope that Dalia placed on the floor, the ruby flames sending lights scattering across the polished stones. "I've been saving this one for quite a while. Ever since I started picking up echoes of Ragnarök entering the atmosphere, I knew it was a matter of time before Baldr brought the fight to us."

My wings flared at that. "Ragnarök and Baldr are here?" I wasn't ready to face them. All I had was a lot of anger and a chewed up pit of Yggdrasil's fruit in my pouch.

Dalia nodded and motioned to the telescope. "You're a Frigg. I built this especially for you."

I looked to Will for reassurance. He knelt and gave me an encouraging smile. "What damage can a little telescope do?"

Narrowing my gaze, I glowered. "When it comes to Norse deities, I wouldn't put anything past her."

Dalia might claim to be on our side, but she'd betrayed me before. If Baldr was coming here, I knew I wouldn't put my bets on the Valkyrie who hadn't even washed her hair in three weeks because the water would just evaporate before it got anywhere near her scalp. Not that I needed to bathe... but being on earth without being able to do earthly things just made me feel even more out of place.

Before I had a chance to stop her, Nina crawled over to us and plucked up the telescope. She frowned and turned it over before looking through the eyepiece. "I don't see anything," she complained before tossing it back down onto the carpet. "Must be broken."

Helena waved her away. "That's because you're a Gina, not a Frigg. The only thing you're good at is making it rain." Nina growled and Helena sighed. "And biting people."

Appeased, Nina smiled. Now that I was getting to know her better, she looked the least like a Valkyrie out of the group. She boasted pointed teeth and her nails were unusually long. I'd just chalked it up to her primal nature, but now that I thought about it, perhaps the reason her nature was primal was because she was a division of Valkyrie I didn't often come across. The Gina weren't permitted to live on Muspelheim. They were the only lineage who revolted against our fiery nature and embraced the opposing element. My mother had once talked about them, looking both fond and melancholy about her distant daughters. "The universe cannot be all fire and heat. There must be balance, and that is why the Valkyrie have the Gina to douse the destruction of our flames when we forget not everything deserves to be burned."

My mother's words made me soften towards Nina. She'd been an outcast long before she'd met her human.

Helena, poised as ever, elegantly extended her arm and offered me the telescope. "Why don't you tell us what you see? I will vouch for Dalia, if that helps to change your mind."

Relenting, I accepted it. "Fine."

Dalia watched me with the intent of a predator as I lifted the eyepiece to my face. Blocking out the watching eyes as best I could, I focused on the end of the scope... and into the swirling black void that ended with the flashing maw of Ragnarök itself.

I saw Baldr, handsome as ever, stepping out onto a platform as he greeted an enormous crowd. I frowned, because as the vision came into focus, I realized that he wasn't on Asgard. The glowing lights and lazy waterfall were part of a sky rise resort just a few blocks down from Dalia's condo. I'd seen it on the television being advertised as the "party to be." I'd just flipped the channel every time, uninterested in a social event with a bunch of humans who'd freak out the moment they saw me.

But in this vision, the humans all wore elegant wings and painted themselves with glittering, metallic layers until the more graceful among them might pass as a Valkyrie if I didn't look too close.

What was Baldr up to?

A single dark spot in the vision caught my attention and I focused on it. My magic worked with the telescope to bring the point at the far end of the venue closer. I drew in a shocked gasp when the darkness cleared, revealing Tyler chained to the platform. He strained against the cuffed restraints, jerking when a flash of glittering black swept through his body like lightning. He cried out as the darkness pierced through his skin, ripping off one of the runes he wore on his flesh.

The crowd was oblivious of him, the air alight with the power akin to Grimhildr's soft reprogramming. There wasn't anyone suffering on the platform. There wasn't a dark form ripping Tyler to shreds before their very eyes. There was only fun and dancing and drinks.

I lowered the telescope and a wave of dizziness swept over me. The hairs on my arms stood on end as my powers as a Frigg hummed. I hadn't even realized I'd been using them. "There's going to be a party."

Iris leaned forward, mesmerizing with her mismatching green and red eye. "The one that's been playing on TV?"

Nina bounced up and down. "Does saving the world include going to a party? Because I'm in."

Helena frowned at Nina. "You really are a Gina, completely hopeless and incapable of taking anything seriously. You don't even know what this means, do you?"

I blinked at her. "Are any of us supposed to know what this means?"

Helena rolled her eyes and waved over her mate.

Daniel seemed to calm her and had she still had wings, they would have settled against the agitation that lifted from her face when he was around. He wrapped an arm around her shoulders, seeming to know the calming effect he had on her. "I think what Helena is trying to say is that Baldr's going to try and set a trap." He gave me a wink. "He didn't count on you having allies."

IT'S JUST A NECKLACE

I'd been both jealous and suspicious of my new roommates ever since Will had started bringing them in. They all seemed so happy and content, whereas I just felt left out and confused.

The guys, especially, were growing into themselves after lifetimes of living a terrible curse. Where Michael had telekinesis, the others began to display signs of supernatural gifts as well. I wasn't sure if it was because they'd tasted Yggdrasil's fruit, or because they'd been freed from a centuries-long curse. Whenever I approached Will about it, he managed to change the subject.

Paul opened up first. I liked him and how easy he was. He was older than the rest of the group, seeming to have been an oddity with the Norn's curse. He'd met

Iris in his late thirties, which also would explain why she looked a bit older to me. Perhaps she was so closely bonded to her mate, she's matched the age of when he was supposed to die.

It still baffled me that all of these men would have died, over and over again, if it hadn't been for Will. As Paul gave me a friendly smile, guilt wafted over me, because I would have given them all up if it'd meant Will would have been safe.

"You've been quite distant," he remarked. We reclined on chairs that looked over the city, resting on a long balcony with the soft breeze slipping through my hair. It was refreshing to be outside. The iron chair beneath me managed my heat and I tried to concentrate on the wind, allowing it to sweep away the worst of my embers. "I just recently lost my mortal body," I said.

He nodded knowingly. "My memories started to return after Will fed me the fruit." He twisted, revealing a long scar along his neck that I hadn't noticed before. "This was given to me when Iris lost her body." He covered it up again with the long layered sweaters he seemed to prefer. Now I knew why. "I've kept it as a birthmark through every life since. It was a burn from one of her feathers when Freya cut off her wings."

I grimaced. "You were there for that?"

He laced his fingers and the only evidence that recalling these memories bothered him was the twitch at his jaw. "Iris should have reaped me during that life, but she didn't. She spared me, and then she broke the Norn's curse." He waved away the memories as if they were a stench that lingered in the air. "Anyway, you can guess the rest. Iris was banished from her home-world and doomed to watch me turn into a vegetable over and over again. All the while trying to live on a planet incompatible with her nature."

I frowned. Even though this planet didn't have molten lava spewing all over the place—for the most part—I wouldn't call it incompatible. "I find it quite nice, actually."

He gave me a weak grin. "I didn't mean the atmosphere. I meant the people. If Iris ever slipped up, Thor would show up and wipe everyone's memories. Even people she'd turned into friends. When I would turn forty years old, that's when I was slated to die or turn into a vegetable. Sometimes I'd take my own life because I knew it was coming. I didn't have the memories, but my heart knew. Other times I'd let the end come, and then she'd have to suffer until I died of old age." He ground his teeth before continuing. "She's had to endure so much worse suffering than I ever did. If she wanted any sort of friendships to get through those rough times, she had to hide who she was, on top of everything else."

I pressed my lips together. "How?"

Taking that as his cue, he struggled to his feet, and I realized his birthmarks weren't just for show, but lasting deformities that caused him pain. "I usually hide it better than this. I must be tired." He gave me a wink. "I'll send Iris in. She'll be glad to teach you, just as she's taught me."

He opened the glass door and called for his mate. She came to him in a flutter of smiles and soft kisses. "Paul. I hope you've been kind to Valerie."

He smiled and cupped her face, giving her a kiss. "Of course." He slipped inside and ushered her out onto the balcony. "Now you two have your girl talk." He jabbed a thumb over his shoulder. "I'm going to play a game with Daniel and wipe that smug smile off his face. He thinks he's some poker god. It's time that someone give him a dose of humility."

I thought Paul was joking around, until I spotted the wicked grin on his face. He had a trick up his sleeve he wasn't telling us about.

"Oh dear," Iris said as she rested her elbows on the rail. "He's going to get us in trouble, isn't he?"

I couldn't help but be put at ease. Iris, with her joyful smile—as if she'd gained the whole world overnight—which, now that I thought about it, is basically what had happened. She'd been living a nightmare for gods knew how long.

Her smile dimmed and she looked back out over the city. "So, this party. What do you think of it?"

I got up and joined her as we leaned along the rail. My wings swayed behind me. My feathers grazed her shoulder, then I jerked it back with a grimace. "Oh, sorry, are you okay?"

She laughed and brushed away the ash, revealing flaw-less skin. "A little touch of home isn't going to hurt me."

I stared at her shoulder where I'd burned off the edge of her blouse. "I feel like a walking inferno. I'm not used to everything around me being so... delicate."

She gave my arm a squeeze and I relaxed. I'd nearly forgotten how much I'd missed touch, just a quick embrace or something as simple as a comforting gesture. "Are you committed to walking into Baldr's trap? Because that's exactly what this party is."

Images of Tyler being drained of his life up on a platform for everyone to see made my stomach churn. "I can't just leave Tyler defenseless." I hadn't told anyone about what I'd seen, but there was something about Iris' softness and friendly bi-colored gaze that made me want to open up to her.

"Tyler," she repeated the name and her brows furrowed. "Why does that name sound so familiar?"

I couldn't remember Iris, but Tyler was a lot older than me. There was no telling what kind of trouble he'd gotten into before he'd become a Valiant. "He was my guardian for a long time. He went by the name 'Tyr.' Before that, he was working under Dalia as a Heimdall."

Her eyes went wide, giving me a glimpse of the silver ring that surrounded her irises. I laughed, because now I understood where she got her name. "I remember now. I met him once when Dalia first found me." Her gaze unfocused as she dug up the ancient memories. "He went by Tyr back then, too. He was the first to help me understand the darkness that powers my sisters. It helped me understand that my suffering could ease Paul's pain. I'm grateful to him."

I raised an eyebrow. "What is it that he showed you?"

She propped her hands on her hips. "He showed me a nifty trick that you're going to need to learn, because if you're really going to this party, we can't have you walking around a crowded venue in your true Valkyrie form."

I frowned. "But it's an angel costume party. The telescope showed me that. I thought the whole point of Baldr's trap was so that I wandered around a crowded venue in my Valkyrie form where he can easily spot me."

Iris shook her head. "We can't do much about your wings and beauty, but that's not what I'm talking about."

Before I could correct her that she was far more beautiful than I could ever be, she tore up a napkin and sprinkled it over my arm. It immediately caught fire and the remaining ash drifted to the ground.

"Oh." She had a point. The moment I bumped up against someone, I'd give them third-degree burns, and any chance of saving Tyler would go up in flames, along with anyone who ventured too close to me.

"As you've seen, we outcasts have learned how to suppress our natural form."

As Iris continued on with the technicalities of how to suppress Muspelheim's raw heat that ran in my blood, I couldn't help but think of what Will had said. I shouldn't deny who and what I was, but if it meant saving Tyler, wasn't it worth it?

"Is it reversible?" I asked. If I did this, I wanted to be able to return to Muspelheim. I didn't belong on earth anymore. Will and I were over, that much was apparent. If I managed to save the universe from the clutches of Ragnarök, I wanted to return to my old life —with some improvements, of course. I hadn't thought too much beyond saving the universe, but as a Frigg, the future was always on my mind. I could teach my sisters how to use their powers without reaping souls. Perhaps I could even find a way to reroute suffering that already existed in the universe and help Freya continue to grow her army while being able to finally put an end to the Norn. I knew the necessity of military might, so I would not deny my mother her daughters. Even if I managed to defeat Ragnarök, Baldr was going to be a permanent, Immortal thorn in my side. I never wanted to be unprepared for him again.

Iris bit her lip before replying to my earlier question. "I'm afraid it's a permanent alteration. This isn't a mortal skin you can just shed. This is your true self that you must change on a fundamental level."

"I know why you did it," I said, my voice lowering. I glanced through the doors and spotted Paul at the table with Daniel. I sensed something supernatural humming through the air and Paul grinned before turning over his cards. Daniel's face flushed red. He opened his mouth to speak, but the glass used in Dalia's condos was akin to one of Ymir's inventions and I couldn't hear a thing. Paul threw his head back with a laugh.

Iris sighed as she watched her mate thoroughly enjoy himself. "He's my everything. When I met him, I just couldn't imagine going back to Muspelheim. I couldn't pretend that reaping a soul was a necessary evil. I'd done it for a long time, but when I met Paul, I just couldn't go through with it."

"Was it love?" I found myself asking. I desperately needed to know if what Will and I had shared was just my imagination, or if he was pushing me away.

She squeezed my arm again. "You know, at first I think it was just our bond, the one that forms between a Valkyrie and her soul. But over time… love grew to replace what we'd both lost." Her gaze flicked to Will who sat at the fireplace with Henry and Michael. Michael used his powers to hover one of the burning logs while Nina clapped her hands. Henry ruffled her hair and even if he hadn't shown signs of his powers yet, he seemed quite content. "You and Will have something, but I think he knows how you feel about Tyler. He's not the kind of guy to stand in the way of what you two had before he was in the picture."

I startled and pulled away from her. "What do you mean? Tyler and I—"

She laughed, the sound musical and gentle on the cool breeze. "I didn't know who your heart belonged to, but it was obvious you've been pining away for some boy out there." She grinned. "Don't worry, sweetheart. We're going to get Tyler back." She offered her hand. "You just have to be willing to have a little faith."

*T*he process to douse the sharp edge of being a Valkyrie wasn't as hard as I'd imagined. All I had to do was rip off my necklace.

I gripped the locket. I'd hardly given it a single thought except for when my mother had used it to remind me I was still under her scrutiny. It burned under my touch, the core of my heat resting inside it.

I'd never questioned that it didn't have a clasp, or that I never took it off. I'd slipped it under any blouse I wore as a mortal, and it had its own space underneath my battle leathers when I was in my Valkyrie form. As a human, it'd kept me grounded, kept all of my Valkyrie's heat strapped safe inside it for when I would shed my mortal skin.

But now… now I gripped it as if I held on for dear life. "I don't know if I can do it," I whispered.

All of the Valkyries had come out onto the balcony when they'd notice embers erupt across my wings. The guys stayed inside and made themselves busy, pretending not to notice that I'd gone into full crises mode.

"You just gotta yank it," Nina said helpfully, jumping up and down with excitement.

Helena glowered at her. "Don't rush her. She has to make the same decision we all did. Even you had a necklace once, even if you didn't live on Muspelheim."

Nina rolled her eyes. "I ripped that thing off so fast. Being a Gina sucked. It's all 'be one with water and fire' my friends," she said, wiggling her fingers. "I got out of there and headed straight for the closest forest. It was a bit of a jog... but can't say I regretted it." She grinned. "Henry was a missionary, you know that? He thought I was some savage that needed his lectures." She winked. "He's lucky he's cute."

As much as I wanted to hear more about Nina's history, Elena gripped my hands. My locket burned underneath my fingertips.

I gazed up into her ruby-rimmed irises. "I'm afraid I'll lose everything," I admitted in a low whisper. If I gave up the deepest part of me just for a chance to save Tyler, what if I was wrong? What if I lost any power to save him just like Baldr wanted, and then Ragnarök devoured the world, all because I acted rashly?

"You're overthinking it," Elena said. "No one is going to make you do anything you don't want to do, and if you ask it of us, we'll go after Baldr ourselves. You don't have to do a thing."

Immediately I shook my head. I couldn't send them off to face Baldr alone. He was a Frigg... just like me. I was the only one who could face him and make it out alive.

"No. This is something I have to do." I closed my eyes and tightened my grip around my necklace. Elena pulled away, but then her hand rested on my arm. Another touch grazed my skin, until all the Valkyries gave me their support with their touch on my blazing skin.

I drew in a deep breath, and then I tore the necklace off my body.

*T*he cascade of unbelievable cold that flooded in to replace the gaping wound in my soul made me gasp.

My sisters gave a collective shudder, but didn't yank away as if they'd known this part was coming.

"Fight through it," Elena offered.

"We're here for you," Iris added.

I opened my eyes and my breath frosted the air and

my teeth chattered. I'd never been so cold in all my life. "W-when does t-this pass?" I asked, my jaw nearly clacking off my face as I tried to speak.

They held on tight, offering me what meager warmth they had to give. "Just a few seconds," Nina said through gritted teeth, and at first I thought she was trying to comfort me, but when she dug her nails into my skin I realized she was talking to herself.

When the sensation of icy daggers passed, leaving me dizzy, the Valkyries helped me inside.

"Make a spot on the sofa," Helena said, barking orders and making sure that the guys adjusted the pillows to perfectly hug my body as they set me down.

Darkness faded in and out of my vision as my consciousness threatened to collapse, then one more familiar touch caressed my cheek.

I fluttered my eyes open to find Will smiling down at me. "Rest, Val. We'll be right here when you wake up."

THE UNKNOWN

For the first time in... ever, I slept in a dreamless sleep. As a Valkyrie, we slept just like mortals did, but as a Frigg I dreamed of different layers in time. A reoccurring dream trapped me in the pits of Muspelheim with gushing lava spewing into a giant cavern, likely a place I'd found myself in when I'd gotten lost playing with Billy in Jotunheim.

Tonight I didn't have my necklace to feed me the constant fuel of my race, and I realized that the fires of Muspelheim didn't come naturally to the Valkyrie. We were Freya's weapons, forged with the hottest of flames.

Without her oppressive guidance, I was left with what I was on my own, which was a ball of determination and emotion, and the Immortal drive of a Frigg scorned.

I awoke to the scent of coffee and waffles. A human breakfast if I'd ever smelled one, but my stomach surprised me with a gurgle of protest that I wasn't jumping off the couch and devouring everything there was to eat right now.

Groaning, I sat up and clutched at my head. In spite of Will's promise, exactly no one was waiting for me when I woke up. Well, Nina was curled in a ball in front of the fireplace, but by the slow rise and fall of her chest, and her slack-jawed posture assured me that nothing short of an explosion was going to move her from that spot.

Feeling sore and stiff, I wobbled to the kitchen and leaned against the doorframe. Everyone had crammed inside, crowding around the bar to find a task to prepare the feast.

Iris spotted me first, her bi-colored gaze flashing with excitement. "She's awake!"

I groaned when they shouted. "Not so loud," I complained. "It feels like I got hit with a boulder."

I flinched away when Will came to my side and moved

to take my arm. My feathers brushed against his face and for a moment I watched him, horrified, just waiting for his beautiful features to scab over with blisters, but nothing happened. Instead he swatted away my feathers with a laugh. "Don't be skittish. You're safe now."

Feeling sheepish, I took his offered hand and let him guide me to the closest stool. Daniel shoved a plate full of delicious food in front of my face. "The girls say you become a little bit mortal when you take off the necklace. That means you need to eat."

Without even asking, I grabbed a fork and shoved half a waffle into my mouth. I groaned. It was so unbelievably delicious.

He slid a bottle of maple syrup. "It's even better with this."

Murmuring my thanks around a mouthful of food, I popped off the cap and doused my waffles with the goop my memories said would be quite sweet and indeed scrumptious. Another mouthful fulfilled that promise and my toes curled.

"How are you feeling?" Will asked.

I tore my gaze away from my food and realized that

the entire room had been watching me gorge myself. I swallowed my final mouthful and dabbed away the crumbs with a napkin. It was nice to be able to use napkins again. "Other than starving and willing to eat my own arm, pretty good." Guilt washed over me. Here I was, indulging, meanwhile Tyler was out there somewhere as Baldr's prisoner. Was he making him suffer even now, or would he save that for the party?

"What day is it?" I asked, suddenly worried I might have slept through the whole thing.

"Relax," Elena said, pushing a glass of orange juice at me. "Gather your strength. The party's tonight."

Another waffle fell onto my plate and I looked up to see Michael grinning at me.

"Do you think she'll be ready?" Helena asked, always practical, as she gave Elena a raised brow. "She slept two days while she was undergoing the change."

"I'm fine," I growled before stabbing my waffle with my fork. Less talking. More food.

Nina joined me with her own plate as she happily ate with her hands. She opted for a plate full of oranges. "I just love fruit," she commented as she split a peel and the scent hit me right in the gut, making me think of Sam.

I continued to eat, but slower this time. Will gave me a pensive look, but I ignored him. I'd already been through so much, and now I could never go back to Muspelheim.

For the first time in my life, I didn't know what the future might hold.

---

*M*ichael had turned on the television and flipped through the channels, only to find all of them talking about Baldr's party.

"You sure he doesn't have a hacked version of Grimhildr?" Helena asked to no one in particular. She sat cross-legged on the couch and frowned at the screen that glowed over the mantle.

Nina, seeming to have formed a bond with Helena, swatted at her ankle—at least as much as Henry would allow. Her mate wrapped his arms around her until she squealed and finally relented, falling into him with a contented growl.

"Why don't you tell us?" Daniel asked Paul with a scowl. "You're the one who can read minds."

Paul grabbed his chest in mock-surprise. "Whatever do you mean?"

Daniel crossed his arms and joined his equally serious mate on the couch. "No one beats me at poker. That's the only way you could have possibly won."

"Shh," I hissed and grabbed the remote from Henry as I turned the volume up.

Abnormal weather reports black-out all over the skies as a strange phenomenon means stargazers will need to take a night off.

The serious reports turned to encouragement that said stargazers should attend Baldr's party. I scoffed and turned off the TV.

"Hey," Michael complained and the remote flung out of my grip of its own accord. He caught it in midair and grinned. "I wasn't finished watching."

"No, Val's right," Will said, standing and offering me his hand. "It's time to make our game plan."

We tallied up our strengths. Paul could read minds and tell us who was working for Baldr and who wasn't. Michael could follow me and react the fastest, taking any weapons out of enemy hands with a mere thought. The other Valkyries would attend, garbed with their own faux-wings Dalia had so kindly contributed. We didn't tell her that Tyler was the star of the show, or else she might have insisted on coming herself—and ruining any efforts at subtlety.

"I appreciate the help," I began, making my third attempt to go it alone. "You don't need to help me, none of you do." I stood at the door with Dalia's outfit for me, something closer to my Valkyrie leathers that hugged me. The gold trim around the waistband was soft against my fingertips and the flowing folds of the dress hugged my thighs all the way down to my heeled boots. Not the best wear for fighting, but it helped me fit in at a human party.

Nina propped her hands on her hips and smiled, although it was more of a show of pointed teeth. "You gave me Henry back. If you think I'm letting you walk into that place alone, you're a neon frog."

When I gave Henry a raised brow, he waved me away.

"Don't ask. She liked to pounce on the poisonous frogs back home and 'test her mettle.'" He scooped her up in his arms and gave her a squeeze. "Regardless, Nina has a point. You gave us our lives back, but we know it's not over yet. That black-out the humans are talking about is Ragnarök, isn't it?"

I hesitated, but all eyes were on me. I nodded.

Helena adjusted one of her fake wings, fussing with Daniel to stop touching it. "Then let's get going." She brushed away invisible dust and then gave me a smile. "Where I come from, fashionably late isn't a thing. You're just late."

Filtering out the door and getting hit by New York's chill air reminded me that I wasn't a daughter of Muspelheim anymore. I shivered and wrapped my feathers around myself. When I noticed Will shivering too, I opened one wing and drew him into the cocoon of warmth.

We bypassed the limo that Dalia had waiting for us. I preferred walking, and I wasn't interested in facing the end of one of her telescopes. If she wanted to spy on us, she'd have to do it from a safe distance. Just the fact that we hadn't heard from her cemented my theory that Dalia couldn't see past Ragnarök's shadows. Tyler was unreachable, even to a goddess and that should have scared me, but I felt like I finally had my head on straight. No matter what happened, I was doing the right thing.

Will's shivers eased as we walked together. He matched my stride and my wing brushed up against his back. The nerves were sensitive, and I wouldn't allow myself to get this close to just anyone, but Will wasn't just anyone. No matter our falling out, I cared deeper about him than I'd ever thought possible.

"What do you think Baldr will try to do, once you're inside, I mean?" he asked.

I didn't know if he was just trying to make conversation or if he was concerned, but there was no sense in lying to him. "He's going to try and bait me with Tyler."

His eyes widened and if it hadn't been from the encouraging shove of my wing, he would have stopped in his tracks. "He's got Tyler?"

I nodded. "He must have breached the Einherjar." I didn't know what that meant for my parents, but if the ancient Norse gods hadn't been able to stop Baldr from coming to earth, then I didn't want to think of what might have happened to them.

There'd been an entire army of Skuld bearing down on the Einherjar when I'd gone to Muspelheim. I shouldn't have abandoned Tyler there to fend for himself, but he'd ordered me to go. There hadn't been any time and Ragnarök was still my greatest threat—at least, I'd thought it was. Now I was beginning to question that. If Ragnarök could be controlled, then it mattered more who was at the helm.

The ground beneath my feet seemed to jump to a low bass that rumbled the streets the closer we ventured to the venue; an old building with a crowd and velvet rope blocking off the entrance. I paused to take in the sheer number of people that spilled out into Central Park. "Wow," I breathed.

Nina jumped up and down, nearly skipping down the street as people started to filter past us. At first I panicked, wondering if Thor would crash down onto us in retaliation of breaching mortals witnessing a Valkyrie in the flesh, but they hooted their marvel at my "costume" and grabbed the edges of wings attached to their back, spreading them and pretending to flap away.

"How are we supposed to get in?" Iris asked, her brow knitting with concern. "There're so many people. The main event can't hold so many."

Will seemed unconcerned. "Baldr wouldn't have gone through all this trouble to lure Val out if he wasn't going to let her inside." He turned to me and leaned in, lowering his voice. "This is where you're on your own, Val, but you have to find a way to get us all inside. Baldr won't expect you to be coming with friends."

I pinched my lips together and nodded, withdrawing my wings to allow Will to back away.

I matched each gaze in return, marveling how I'd made such close friends in such a short time. Paul smiled. "You can say it out loud, Val. The others would like to hear it."

Iris punched him in the ribs in punishment for reading my mind and he doubled-over, but I was already smiling.

"Paul's right," I said. "I've grown to care about all of you, and you care about me, even though I don't think I deserve it." I straightened and a breeze kicked away my metallic locks. I drew in a deep breath of New York's crisp night air. Something else was on the breeze. The tangy blood-sweet scent of Ragnarök drew close. "Even as a Frigg, I can't tell you the outcome of tonight. All I can say is that I know Baldr intends to use Tyler, and if he succeeds, Ragnarök will be unstoppable."

I glanced at Will, hoping to sense if there was any spike of bitterness or jealousy, but I only sensed his calm resolve to help me in any way he knew how.

We marched on, myself in the lead and the array of my allies trailing behind me. When I reached the bouncer, I did a double take.

Shade, one of Dalia's men and a friend of Tyler. He gave me a grim-faced greeting. "Thought you might be here. Dalia sent me to make sure you gained entry." He unlocked the velvet rope and glanced over my shoulder. "Brought your friends, too?"

Tyler had warned me never to tell Shade who I was, but it sounded like word had somehow gotten out. I was the reason that Tyler had become a Valiant in the first place. He'd fought his Heimdall heritage any way he'd known how, and that included selling his soul to Odin, my father, for a chance to quell the misery of his curse. Each soul Freya fed him added another scar to his collection, and another promise that he would take the darkness in my stead.

I sensed the darkness now, its pull stronger without the purging fires of Muspelheim to keep it at bay. It called to me, whispered for me to reunite with Tyler and accept Ragnarök's cold embrace.

I shook my head and faced Shade. "Yes, we are all looking to get inside." I bit my lip before adding, "Tyler's in there. Whatever Baldr has told you, he plans on killing him and taking this whole planet down next."

Shade's face paled. He reminded me of Tyler in the way his midnight hair fell into his eyes and he had that kind of murderous look that was sexy all at the same time. He leaned in close. "I know. Baldr thinks he paid me off with a couple of vials of Yggdrasil sap." He shoved a vial into my hand. "Take it, and get rid of that bastard."

I closed my fingers around the prize and grimly nodded.

Flaring my wings, which awarded oohs and aahs from the crowd thinking I boasted some mechanical garb, I stepped into the darkness and prepared myself for the one thing I'd never faced before… the unknown.

RAGNARÖK

*D*arkness swarmed inside the venue so thick that I couldn't even make out the crowd farther than a few feet in front of my face. Music thrummed and made the people sway as if it locked them into a trance. Wings moved, making me feel like I was in some kind of nightmare with the undead Valkyries of Muspelheim. My breath caught, expecting for Sam to launch out at me at any second and thrust accusations of my failure in my face.

A gentle touch at my arm brought me back to awareness. Will, flanked by our new allies, moved through the shadows. "You can do this," he whispered, then blended in with the crowd.

I hated how quickly I lost them and my fingers clutched at the empty space at my nape. I wilted. My necklace was gone and for the first time, I was going to have to do this on my own.

Then I heard a cry, the same one from my nightmarish vision that had brought me here. The shadows flashed as they surged with new power, and I spotted Tyler for just a split second before the platform went dark.

His gaze had met mine, and in that split second I knew what he was telling me to do.

Aerie... get out of here.

I wasn't going to listen to him and I clenched my fists as raw determination swept through me. I marched straight towards the platform. Pain ricocheted across my face when I slammed into an invisible wall and a chuckle sounded on the speakers.

"Well, sister, so glad you've decided to join us. I was just thinking your boyfriend was a poor excuse for a snack. Ragnarök would truly become unstoppable if I fed it a Frigg."

I slammed my fist against the invisible wall, awarding myself only strange looks from surrounding patrons who danced in a daze. When they refused to move, I shoved them out of the way with my wings.

Baldr appeared on the edge of the platform and

grinned, looking manic and wild with his hair sticking out at all angles. Apparently using hair gel was his idea of a fashion statement. "I'm so disappointed that you haven't decided to join me. It's unfortunate, but I can rebuild this world with or without you." His grin widened. "Unfortunately, I'll have to destroy it before there's something worthy to rebuild. That's where your boyfriend comes in handy." Another male scream overrode the music and I beat against the wall as rage took over. Even without Muspelheim's link, my vision tinged with red. "Let him go and perhaps I won't kill you," I snapped.

He buckled over and held his stomach as he laughed. "You really are my sister. Arrogant and oblivious to the very end."

Before I could retort, someone bumped into me from behind. I blinked at Paul.

He pretended to be drunk and laughed, tangling with my wings as we both tumbled to the ground. "He's terrified," he said, just loud enough that the music drowned out his words from anyone else who might be listening. "He's fed Ragnarök too much, and now it's out of control. Tyler is the only thing keeping it in check, but when it's done feeding on him, it's going to come after the next most powerful object."

I swallowed hard. Baldr had managed to unlatch Ragnarök from Muspelheim, meaning it'd already devoured what was left of the undead Valkyrie and the power offered by the planet's core. I could only hope that the Surtr still huddled in the protection of Jotunheim and I hadn't been too late. But now Ragnarök was here, and if Tyler was the only thing distracting it, the next most powerful object in Ragnarök's vicinity would either be Baldr... or me.

"And how many souls have you fed on?" I asked, shooting to my feet. "If I'm so oblivious, then why can I see you shaking?"

His spine shot rigid at my taunt, rage tinting his expression with a mixture of surprise. That's exactly the kind of reaction I'd been going for.

I used his hesitation to slam into the invisible wall again, because I knew it was some magic of his own creation. It hummed and dipped with the wrongness that reeked of his power. All I needed to do was break his concentration long enough to get through the barrier.

I didn't have to know that Michael was behind me. His mental shove sent me reeling into the wall hard enough for my head to spin… and to form a hairline crack.

Baldr snarled with primal rage and snapped his fingers, enacting the first round of his attack.

Half the crowd shifted before my very eyes. Flesh melted away, revealing the horror of the Skuld and their white bones shining through shadow. The other enemy was one I hadn't encountered before. Ice creatures with faces frosting over with splintered eyes screeched and the high-pitched cry made me buckle to my knees. Then I recalled the race of Jotun that had betrayed the gods long ago. The Skaoi, ice elementals that had settled in the folds of Neptune and likewise inhospitable planets frozen to the core—just like their hearts.

The crowd exploded and my Valkyrie allies launched into action, forming a barricade around me as I worked on the barrier.

A flash, another cry, and Tyler yanking at his chains. I had to hurry. This was the part of my vision that, if it came to fruition, meant Ragnarök would get exactly what it needed to become unstoppable.

"You are only making this worse!" I shouted. Rage tinted my vision red and I found the strength to summon my spear. I was so grateful that the weapon wasn't attached to the necklace I'd detached from my body and my soul. I wasn't a daughter of fire anymore, but I was still a Valkyrie; I was still a weapon that would seek justice.

I pierced the crack in the barrier with my blade and steadied my foot on the wall as I levered it back and forth. I thrust my wings to give me balance as I worked.

"You know nothing of Ragnarök!" Baldr bellowed, but I recognized the tinge of panic in his voice. "I've studied it all my life. What have you done? Played footsie with a Valiant and a human. You're pathetic."

I slammed the spear into the crack again and the barrier finally fell. I glanced over my shoulder once to check on my friends. They were holding off the attack, but just barely. Nina clawed at the face of one of the Skaoi, sending ice splintering everywhere. Red tinged the floor, betraying that not all humans had survived the onslaught. Michael levitated one of the Skuld in the air, containing the wisps of violent darkness before flinging it at another. Its neighbor invaded one of the humans, sending the man roaring towards Will. Will punched the man in the face and it went down, sending the Skuld unravelling with him. He glanced at me over his shoulder and gave me a nod.

I had to let them fight, and while they did their job, I had to do mine. I spread my wings and I did what a Valkyrie does best.

I launched, spear in hand, straight towards my enemy.

---

*B*aldr grinned, and I knew at the last moment that I'd made a mistake.

He vanished, leaving me to fly face-first into yet another barrier. This time it snapped around me with finality and I found myself embraced by a familiar glittering darkness.

A male groan drew my attention and I crawled across broken glass until my fingers met chains.

I dismissed my spear in a puff of flame and ran my touch over the iron until I found ice-cold skin.

"Tyler?" I whispered, the word a desperate plea.

His hand gripped me with unexpected strength. "Aerie," he responded and the shadows cleared just enough for me to see his bloodied and bruised face. "You shouldn't have come here. It's a—"

I waved him away. "Yeah, yeah. It's a trap. I got that."

He smirked and my toes curled. Even now, with chaos rampaging all around us and certain doom hanging above our heads, he could make my breath catch with one of his wry grins. Then his gaze fell to my collarbone and his eyes went wide. "You don't have your necklace." His eyes shot back up. "You gave that up... for me?"

I swallowed hard. Of course I had. The only hesitation had been if it would be enough to save him, and now I wasn't so sure. Yet, as I wrapped my fingers around his and felt my heart slide into place alongside his, I knew that choosing Tyler would never be the wrong choice. "I couldn't just let you suffer."

He drew me in close and buried his face in my neck. He inhaled as if I was air itself and he'd drown without me. "Aerie. You're a beautiful fool."

Ice spread around my knees and a piercing cold made my legs go numb. "What is that?" I asked as a vibrant hum sounded all around us.

He held me tighter. "You don't have your mother to protect you anymore. Ragnarök can feed on you now."

Just before the glittering black descended on us, I drew out the vial that Shade had given me. I popped off the cork and downed it in one shot.

Heat blasted through me and my wings flared out with renewed embers. My eyes went wide, because this wasn't just some harvested sap from a Huldra honeycomb nest. This was the same stuff that had made up unadulterated Yggdrasil fruit.

I didn't question where Baldr had gotten his hands on such a rare and precious commodity—then again, he was a Frigg as well. It shouldn't have surprised me that he'd made his single trip to Yggdrasil and grabbed a fruit or two. He'd even found a way to harvest it into vials, enough to bribe Immortal bouncers to make sure the right people got into his "end of the world party."

Ragnarök wailed with such agony as it slammed into me, then bounced right back off. It wasn't just the power of Yggdrasil that gave me the strength to withstand its blow, but my acceptance of Tyler's hand in mine. His dark runes stood out stark against the pale marble skin of his body. Corded muscles boasted the scars and they slid over his knuckles and onto me. He'd taken on the shadows of the world for far too long. It was time that I accepted what I was. It was time that I accepted the dark connection that Tyler and I shared.

I stood, hand-in-hand with Tyler, as my skin glowed to life. The flames of Muspelheim renewed in me three-fold and shadows scurried away from my feet. Ice melted and the air steamed as I blazed. "I am your commander!" I bellowed up at the writhing void.

The glitter inside of Ragnarök's dark mass twinkled like a thousand stars, and now I knew what they were. Each diamond speck was a lost soul, a piece of a heart torn asunder and bound with so much suffering that it would never find peace. Ragnarök was a poor, pitiful creature that only knew how to devour, to destroy, all in an attempt to rid itself of its sorrow.

"Freya has trapped you for millennia and made your suffering grow," I said, my voice lowering.

The mass crooned and bellowed, snaps of black ice whipping around my face. It wasn't going to try to feed on me again, now while I glowed with the strength of a hundred suns. It lowered as if trying to get a better look at me and I stared, face-to-face, looking into the eyes of the underworld.

A thousand voices permeated my mind as Ragnarök tried to talk to me. In there somewhere was Sam, my lost sisters, even Will's mother. They all just wanted the suffering to end and my wings flared with embers at the distaste their rot left in my mouth.

There was only one way to save them. Only one way I'd been trained to deal with lost causes and enemies.

I summoned my spear and I slashed.

---

*R*agnarök split in two and the wound I'd left behind glowed with a bright scar of purification and light. The blackness cracked all around, sending streaks of lightning followed by ear-breaking thunder to crash through the building. The upper floor peeled away in the crash of a tornado that hadn't quite touched down, leaving me an open view of the star-speckled sky.

Across Central Park humans cried out and the skies churned in response to their suffering. I swept out a hand, my powers as a Frigg humming to life as I slowed time for them.

The world kept spinning. Ragnarök continued to fall apart, but at least those impacted by the rampaging screams of chaos wouldn't have to endure it for much longer. I protected each one in a bubble of their own present moment, a gift that Will had taught me.

I banished what was left of Ragnarök to the low weight of the space-time net. With Yggdrasil's power running through my veins, I connected with the universe on a level I'd never experienced before. I knew its layers and its secrets and where Ragnarök could find its own present in time, away from suffering, away from worlds it only knew how to destroy.

When it was gone, I released my time stop on the humans. Distant groans sounded, followed by the low hum of Grimhildr kicking in for cleanup. I straightened, because surely that meant that Freya was still alive. And if she was, why had she left me to fend off Ragnarök all by myself?

Tyler spoke to my unanswered questions, showing no shame that he could read my mind. "Your parents love you more than you know," he said, his fingers wrapping around my chin and pulling me up to him. "Please don't hurt, Aerie."

Tears sizzled in my eyes and I was so grateful that Tyler could withstand my heat as a Valkyrie renewed. I couldn't bear to be without his touch just now. "Are they dead?"

A slow nod and my stomach dropped. "When Baldr sent you to earth... Odin activated the Mojinir."

My vision blurred, my tears coming too fast for my heat to wipe them out.

Muspelheim was gone. That's why Mojinir had come to earth. Odin had activated his last resort, destroying the planet so Ragnarök couldn't get any stronger. If he hadn't, I might never have been able to subdue it.

"But, I'm a Valkyrie," I said, the words not making logical sense. All I could think of was that I had nowhere to call home anymore. I was orphaned, alone. "Where will I go?"

He leaned in closer until our breaths mingled. "Aerie, my love. You are the Queen of Asgard."

The shock that came with that statement didn't prepare me for the full force of his kiss that he was no longer able to keep at bay. He crushed his mouth to mine and wound his arms around me to squeeze me close. His fingers tangled with my feathers, the sensitive nerves lighting up under his touch.

I returned his kiss with every ounce of fervor I'd denied myself before. Tyler had always been the one. He'd always been there for me and always held my heart.

"*R*agnarök has been vanquished!" shouted Billy, who'd become my new overseer for matters concerning Asgardian management.

The crowds loved him. The Surtr had enough charm to go along with his wit and most importantly, his voice carried with undiluted adoration of his new queen.

It felt weird to be a queen, but as I sat on the throne with a wide back to accommodate my wings, Tyler slipped his fingers through mine, a stolen touch to help me feel grounded and in control.

Whenever we touched, our shadows mingled and his dark runes quivered over his body. Our love wouldn't bring about the end of the world... it would save it.

He grinned, and even though an entire city cheered and a purple sky danced above us, it felt like we were on our own little planet in our own rotating solar system, where he was the moon and I was the sun, forever revolving around one another in an endless cycle.

"Are you happy?" he asked as his fingers ran up my arm and he gave my wing a strong caress.

I shivered at the possessive touch. Tyler was mine, and I was his. I didn't care if everyone knew it. His internal glow radiated. He was free of Odin's bond and his dark runes gleamed on his bare skin covered only by a sheer, parted shirt. He preferred it this way, even if his corded muscles and rough lines running into a tight waistband made my cheeks permanently red. This was him, son of the Heimdall line and survivor of Ragnarök, his scars and suffering proudly on display. The sharp angles of his face as he gave me a wry smile broke any resolve I might have had, and I gravitated to him until our lips met and I answered his question the only way I knew how. I kissed him, wrapping my wings around us to give us a shield of privacy.

When I came up for breath, he laughed and his hands roamed my face. "Aerie. I'm happy too."

*A*sgard had its new queen and Will eventually revealed to me what power it was he'd gained after accepting Yggdrasil's fruit.

The power to read hearts.

It wasn't like Paul who read literal thoughts. Will's power went so much deeper, reading intent and truth that even people couldn't admit to themselves.

A truth such as a certain Valkyrie having always loved Tyler.

Will and I had been bonded by a supernatural magic designed to bring Valkyrie and Soul together, a trusting relationship that was necessary for the reaping. I'd seen that bond turn into love with the outcasts, but as much as Will and I cared for one another, he'd been right. Our bond was a mixture of friendship and duty. He'd never deserved the curse placed on him, and I hadn't deserved the responsibility put on my shoulders. We'd managed to undo the hardships bound to us, but not without sacrifice and pain. He knew that my heart belonged to Tyr, and that it always would, which was why his sacrifice to push me away was the greatest one of all.

I watched him through one of Dalia's telescopes from time to time. Perhaps that's a bit creepy, but I wanted to make sure he was okay. I watched him grow; becoming a leader to the gifted men he'd saved with Yggdrasil's fruit. Dalia's Huldra also bonded with him, listened to him, and the vacuum left behind by the end of the Norse gods quickly filled with his charisma and candor.

Tonight he slipped away into Central Park as I'd seen him do a thousand times. There was a particular Huldra he'd been courting for some time now. It didn't surprise me that the carefree creatures were the only ones who could get him to come out of his shell. When his lips lowered onto a girl with frosted green leaves forming a crown at her brow, I smiled, glad he could find happiness, and lowered my telescope as I returned to my own life on Asgard where we built our family—and a new army.

Baldr had disappeared that night Ragnarök had been vanquished. There'd been no sign of Dalia either, and I wondered if they'd been sucked in by the massive sink Ragnarök had created during its departure, or if something more sinister was at play.

For Tyler's sake, I hoped his mother had survived.

For now, I stood out on my balcony and spread my wings, allowing my feathers to catch the warm sun's rays. Tyler's hands wrapped around my waist and his lips went to my neck, sending new shivers down my spine.

"Is everything all right?" he asked, his voice low and scratchy from sleep.

I wrapped my arms over his and indulged in the mixture of heat and ice he always stirred inside of me. Separated, we were just two broken souls. Together, we were healed, our rough edges sealing together until we became one.

"Everything is absolutely perfect."

THE END

Thank you for reading the third and final installment of Valkyrie Allegiance!

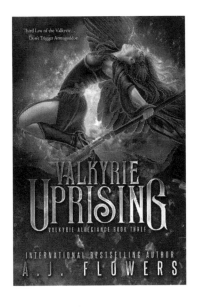

Please take a moment to leave a review on your favorite online retailer and help A.J. reach more readership. Reviews are critical for indie authors, so every click counts! It doesn't have to be much! "Loved it!" will do!

You can help A.J. by reviewing her books on Goodreads, Bookbub, and Online Retailers.

Be sure to join the A.J. Newsletter to be informed of new releases by going to AJ-Flowers.com!

Also by A.J. Flowers

Book 1 in the Dweller Saga
Cats have a thousand lives. Since I'm on my last one…
I better make it count.

Celestial Downfall: The Complete Trilogy
You've Never Seen Angels and Demons Like This
Angels have ruled the world for too long... It'll take
one of their own to stop their reign.

Made in the USA
Middletown, DE
05 August 2022